John Creasey – Mast

Born in Surrey, England in 1908 into were nine children, John Creasey grew up to be a true master story teller and international sensation. His more than 600 crime, mystery and thriller titles have now sold 80 million copies in 25 languages. These include many popular series such as *Gideon of Scotland Yard*, *The Toff*, *Dr Palfrey* and *The Baron*.

Creasy wrote under many pseudonyms, explaining that booksellers had complained he totally dominated the 'C' section in stores. They included:

Gordon Ashe, M E Cooke, Norman Deane, Robert Caine Frazer, Patrick Gill, Michael Halliday, Charles Hogarth, Brian Hope, Colin Hughes, Kyle Hunt, Abel Mann, Peter Manton, J J Marric, Richard Martin, Rodney Mattheson, Anthony Morton and *Jeremy York*.

Never one to sit still, Creasey had a strong social conscience, and stood for Parliament several times, along with founding the One Party Alliance which promoted the idea of government by a coalition of the best minds from across the political spectrum.

He also founded the British Crime Writers' Association, which to this day celebrates outstanding crime writing. The Mystery Writers of America bestowed upon him the Edgar Award for best novel and then in 1969 the ultimate Grand Master Award. John Creasey's stories are as compelling today as ever.

INPECTOR WEST SERIES

Inspector West Takes Charge
Inspector West Leaves Town (Also published as: Go Away to Murder)
Inspector West at Home (Also published as: An Apostle of Gloom)
Inspector West Regrets
Holiday for Inspector West
Battle for Inspector West
Triumph for Inspector West (Also published as: The Case Against Paul Raeburn)
Inspector West Kicks Off (Also published as: Sport for Inspector West)
Inspector West Alone
Inspector West Cries Wolf (Also published as: The Creepers)
A Case for Inspector West (Also published as: The Figure in the Dusk)
Puzzle for Inspector West (Also published as: The Dissemblers)
Inspector West at Bay (Also published as: The Case of the Acid Throwers)
A Gun for Inspector West (Also published as: Give a Man a Gun)
Send Inspector West (Also published as: Send Superintendent West)
A Beauty for Inspector West (Also published as: The Beauty Queen Killer)
Inspector West Makes Haste (Also published as: Murder Makes Haste)
Two for Inspector West (Also published as: Murder: One, Two, Three)
Parcels for Inspector West (Also published as: Death of a Postman)
A Prince for Inspector West (Also published as: Death of a Assassin)
Accident for Inspector West (Also published as: Hit and Run)
Find Inspector West (Also published as: Doorway to Death)
Murder, London - New York
Strike for Death (Also published as: The Killing Strike)
Death of a Racehorse
The Case of the Innocent Victims
Murder on the Line
Death in Cold Print
The Scene of the Crime
Policeman's Dread
Hang the Little Man
Look Three Ways at Murder
Murder, London - Australia
Murder, London - South Africa
The Executioners
So Young to Burn
Murder, London - Miami
A Part for a Policeman
Alibi (Also published as: Alibi for Inspector West)
A Splinter of Glass
The Theft of Magna Carta
The Extortioners
A Sharp Rise in Crime

Sport for Inspector West

(Inspector West Kicks Off)

John Creasey

Copyright © 1949 John Creasey Literary Management Ltd.
© 2014 House of Stratus

All rights reserved. No part of this publication may be reproduced, stored in a retrieval system, or transmitted, in any form, or by any means (electronic, mechanical, photocopying, recording, or otherwise), without the prior permission of the publisher. Any person who does any unauthorised act in relation to this publication may be liable to criminal prosecution and civil claims for damages.

The right of John Creasey to be identified as the author of this work has been asserted.

This edition published in 2014 by House of Stratus, an imprint of Stratus Books Ltd., Lisandra House, Fore Street, Looe, Cornwall, PL13 1AD, U.K.
www.houseofstratus.com

Typeset by House of Stratus.

A catalogue record for this book is available from the British Library and the Library of Congress.

ISBN 07551-3582-2
EAN 978-07551-3582-0

This book is sold subject to the condition that it shall not be lent, resold, hired out, or otherwise circulated without the publisher's express prior consent in any form of binding, or cover, other than the original as herein published and without a similar condition being imposed on any subsequent purchaser, or bona fide possessor.

This is a fictional work and all characters are drawn from the author's imagination. Any resemblance or similarities to persons either living or dead are entirely coincidental.

Chapter One

The Bliss of Ignorance

Guy Randall had no idea that he was going to die.

There was no reason why he should. No normal man of thirty-three expects death to be lurking round the corner.

What he did on the day of his death is of importance for two reasons. It gave the CID three weeks of intensive work to find out exactly where he went and whom he saw; for probably one of the people with whom he talked, some hours before the fatal moment, was his murderer.

Even apart from its climax, it was an unusual day for Randall; in its way, exciting and stimulating. He was happy, eager and energetic, and felt very fit; and he turned many corners before taking that final, fatal step.

Chief Inspector Roger West of New Scotland Yard, who retraced those steps with infinite patience, was eventually able to present to his superiors a complete, comprehensive account of Randall's movements, but he couldn't supply them with a schedule of his thoughts.

West's report started from the early morning of the last day of Randall's life.

The room was neither large nor small, but bright because on that March morning the sun was streaming through an open window. It was a room on the second floor of *Maybank,* a Victorian villa in St. John's Wood, and as much a home as a boarding-house can ever be.

Randall slept heavily.

Footsteps sounded outside, and there was a timid tap at the door. After a pause, the tap was repeated, but much more loudly. Randall did not stir, and the door opened; a cup and saucer chinked on a metal tray. A girl, of seventeen or eighteen, came in and spoke: *"It's eight o'clock, Mr Randall!"*

He started, blinked.

"Eh? Oh, hallo." He yawned widely and stretched his arms. "Hallo," he repeated. "'Morning. Wass the time?"

"Nearly eight o'clock," said the girl.

"Time to get up," said Randall, and the girl went out, closing the door behind her.

Breakfast at *Maybank* was an informal meal, and Randall alone of the seven boarders came down at half-past eight. There were two letters and a folded copy of the *Daily Telegraph* by his plate, and as he examined the letters the girl came in with his porridge. He gave her an absent smile and opened the first letter.

It was from his sister, brief and to the point:

'Dear Guy, I'm delighted to hear you're engaged. Every good wish, my dear. When are you going to bring your Sybil to see us? She sounds delightful. Mustn't stay now, I'm so busy, but I had to write something the moment I had your letter. Love, Jane.'

Randall grinned, put the letter down and ate his porridge. He was deep in the second letter when the girl came in again, bringing him a sausage and some fried tomatoes.

The other letter was longer and typewritten. It read:

'My dear Guy. So the misogynist has fallen, the woman-hater becomes the lover! Good – I knew that it was bound to happen some day. No, of course not, this won't affect business at all – why on earth should it? You'll have even more incentive to sell our goods! Whether your wife will be particularly cheerful because you'll be away so often isn't my affair, thank heavens! That brings me to the point of the letter and the point in yours which obviously most worries you. The firm can't, at the moment, give you an office of your own, for there's no vacancy. On the other hand, I'm told that Lewis is talking of retiring, and when he does, the Midlands area will fall vacant. There isn't much doubt that you will get this, and with it the extra £200 a year that it carries. So little doubt, in fact, that the board will increase your stipend by the said £200pa from the date of your wedding. I've written to you at the office today; by the way – try to keep your head out of the clouds long enough to see Perriman's. If you could clinch their order – but you won't, of course, they're the most difficult prospects we have. Still, since they've asked for a quotation for their boxes for the next 6 months, we must have a shot at it. I've told you in the other letter you can cut each quotation by 5%, but between you and me, if you can get the order by cutting the quotations by 10 or even 12½%, there wouldn't be any argument here! They've had the quotations, of course. I'll be seeing you! As ever, Jim.'

By the time Randall had finished reading this letter his breakfast was getting cold. He ate quickly, had two more cups of tea and several pieces of toast generously spread with butter and marmalade, then went into the hall. His gloves were in the hall-stand drawer – he didn't wear a hat.

He had to turn two corners before he reached his garage and got out his twelve-horse-power Mitchell saloon. When he drove away, he turned a dozen corners in succession – more when he was in the West End. At half-past nine he turned the last corner before parking his car, then walked to the offices of the Crown Printing and Manufacturing Company, which were in a side-street off the Strand.

Randall hadn't any friends in the London office. When he was travelling in London or the South, it was his business headquarters, and he knew the clerks and the typists by name; they knew him as the star salesman of the Southern Area. He made the hearts of the younger girls flutter because he was good-looking and friendly, but he did nothing to encourage them. Coleman, the office manager and Southern Region Sales Manager, was a middle-aged man. He was already in his office. When Randall entered, he pushed aside a letter he was reading and said: "Good morning, I hear I have to congratulate you."

"How the dickens did you know that?" demanded Randall.

Coleman laughed. "Mr Wilson mentioned it in a letter from the works," he said. "There's a letter for you, too, about Perriman's, but you'll never do anything there. Tucktos are dug in too deep. Very glad to hear your news, though. Do I know the lady?"

"No," said Randall. "I met her at Brighton in the summer. We're going to get married very quietly at the end of next week." He looked bright-eyed and happy, and Coleman smiled as if to himself. "You know more about Perriman's and Tucktos than anyone, I should think," Randall went on. "Give me the low-down, will you?"

Coleman did so, and did not hide the fact that he considered it was a forlorn hope.

The Crown Printing and Manufacturing Company manufactured a great variety of articles in paper and cardboard, and had recently experimented successfully with plastic in some of their products. Tucktos, who manufactured patent folding boxes and envelopes, was a much larger firm and had been established fifty years; during practically all that time, they had supplied Perriman's with their requirements – and the requirements were vast.

Perriman's Packed Products used cartons and containers in almost unlimited quantities; they dealt in prepared foodstuffs, they had a vast wholesale business and a chain of retail stores, and in most of their business habits they were ultra-conservative. Few box-making companies had succeeded in obtaining even a share of their custom. The Tucktos company was a combine with different works specialising in producing different boxes, packets, and containers, and the size of the concern enabled them to keep prices down.

Randall had already known a lot of this; Coleman told him much more, and added: "It isn't only the size of Tucktos, you know. They've a fine sales organisation. Know Jeremiah Scott?"

"Yes, I know Jeremiah of Tucktos," said Randall with a faint smile. "Half-rogue, half-genius. He and I are by way of becoming rivals over some prospects, you know. If I take an order away from him, he always gets back on me by wheedling one from people I thought were safe for us. As a matter of fact, Coleman, I'd appreciate your advice about how to tackle that. No one in the business knows more about it than you."

"Very nice of you," murmured Coleman. "What's worrying you?"

"I wouldn't exactly say worrying, but … well, I can't put a finger on it, it's more a feeling than anything else. Jeremiah Scott and I cross each other's paths so much, especially down here, in the South. He always gives me the impression that he's out to cut my throat."

"You mean, he doesn't like you personally?" asked Coleman.

"I don't know about that. He's usually genial enough. I don't often see him unless we happen to be staying at the same hotel, and in the evenings he's generally sozzled. I've never known a man drink like he does."

"I shouldn't think he gets actually drunk," said Coleman judicially. "He can carry his liquor. Tucktos never did like competition, and we've taken quite a lot of business away from them in the past two years. You have particularly. I wouldn't put it past their board to have instructed Jeremiah Scott to go after your business, to try to get you down. But it isn't personal, Randall, if that's what you're afraid of."

"I sometimes wonder," said Randall. "Not that it matters, but I'd like to know how to handle Scott."

"Just do your job," said Coleman, rather smugly. "You won't go far wrong. You may meet Scott again today. Head Office has fixed your appointment for three o'clock, by the way."

"Then Scott will probably have been there this morning," said Randall with a grimace.

He stayed at the office until half-past ten, made three calls between then and twelve-fifteen, getting two quite substantial orders, and then drove to Sibley's, a small, exclusive restaurant in a narrow turning off Charing Cross Road. He had to park his car on a bombed-site parking-place and walked the last hundred yards.

Louis, the commissionaire, who was standing at the corner, turned round, and nearly bumped into a girl.

"Oh!" exclaimed the girl. Her face was pale and her eyes bright, almost frightened. "Oh – Guy!"

"Sybil, darling! What—what's the matter?"

"Oh, nothing. I was afraid I was late."

"So was I." Randall laughed as he took her arm. "Instead, we're both on the dot. Darling, I've the most wonderful news for you?"

"Really, Guy?" The fear, if it had ever been there, faded from the girl's eyes. Louis watched them thoughtfully, smilingly. They hadn't even noticed him.

They went into the gloomy entrance lobby of Sibley's, still arm-in-arm. And it occurred to Louis that he had never seen the girl in such a hurry before, and had noticed that she was looking over her shoulder as she came towards the restaurant. A man turned back when she met Randall. Vaguely, Louis wondered if she'd been hurrying from this man.

Inside, Randall was talking as they followed a waiter to a reserved corner table.

"Yes, it's grand news. I had a letter from Jim this morning – Jim Wilson, my friend on the board."

"Yes, darling, I know who you mean."

"He's turned up absolutely trumps. Practically promised me the Midlands area within a short time, and as a wedding present, two hundred a year extra. Pretty good?"

"Wonderful!"

The waiter came up, was consulted, advised, and went off again. The wine-waiter was also consulted; he advised a red wine and departed.

"Yes," said Randall, gripping Sybil's hand quite openly. He spoke quietly, however, and she had to lean forward to hear his words. "That means a thousand a year salary, darling, and at the rate of commission I've been earning this past year, between two and two and a half thousand a year is certain. Think you can manage on that?"

"Manage!" echoed Sybil. "Guy, it's glorious."

"We're going places," said Randall in a louder voice. "You needn't worry about that, darling – we're in the money!"

The waiter brought hors-d'oeuvre for Sybil, pâté for Guy.

It was half-past two before they left, Sybil to return to her office in the Strand, Randall to go to Perriman's.

The food-products people had a huge building in the City, within hailing distance of the Guildhall. Randall had to give his name to a uniformed commissionaire, who telephoned to Samuel Perriman, the director who was in charge of the buying. Usually callers were escorted to their destination; only a favoured few were allowed to make their own way – and this was the first time Randall had been asked to go up alone. He smiled brightly and said, "Oh yes," quite confidently when the commissionaire asked if he knew where Mr Samuel's office was.

Randall went up in a lift to the fourth of six floors, but when he stepped on to the landing, he hesitated, looking right and left. A diminutive boy came from a huge office with glass doors. When he saw Randall hesitating, he came up and smiled.

"Can I help you, sir?"

"I'm looking for Mr Perriman's office – Mr *Samuel's* office," corrected Randall. "It is on this floor, isn't it?"

"That's right, sir. Along there"—the boy pointed—"first right and then second left, you'll see the name on the door, sir.

Second left.
He turned the corner – and for the second time that day almost ran into someone else. But this time it was a man – a man who backed away and, recognising him, grinned; or leered.
It was Jeremiah Scott.

Chapter Two

The Last Corner

Jeremiah Scott didn't move aside, and Randall had no room to pass. Randall managed an insincere smile. Scott's eyes, glittering bright and bloodshot in the corners, had a bold insolence, calculated to annoy and to hurt.

Randall broke the silence.

"Hallo, Scott."

"Fancy seeing you," jeered Scott. "You're only just too late."

At that moment a door opened and a man appeared. He was a stranger to Randall, but he said, "Good afternoon, Mr Scott," so he obviously knew the Tucktos man. Scott nodded and moved aside.

"I expect we'll be running across each other again," he said to Randall. "So long."

He went off, a tall, broad man with an ungainly walk.

The man who had come out of the office said, "I shouldn't take any joke of Mr Scott's too seriously, Mr Randall." Then he walked on, and Randall was left alone. He glanced after the man, and then went a little farther along the passage, until he reached a door marked '*Mr Samuel Perriman.*' He tapped, and the door was opened promptly by a short, dumpy girl in a black suit and a white blouse.

"Mr Randall?" she asked.

"Yes, I'm Mr Randall."

"Will you please come in?"

She stood aside for him to enter a small office.

"Mr Samuel won't keep you a moment," said the girl, and she went into the next room.

Randall heard Samuel Perriman grunt.

This office had two desks, two typewriters, three filing cabinets, a dictaphone machine, and a 'talking box.' Nothing adorned the panelled walls except two photographs. The photographs were familiar to Randall – but then, they were familiar to every man and woman in Great Britain and in many places abroad. The woman was middle-aged, smiling, somehow a 'type' – comfortable, competent, the epitome of middle-class contentment.

The man was a little older, a Judge Hardy of a man, with greying hair and a tired but friendly smile; he looked as if he were sitting back in an easy chair after a hard day at the office. The remarkable thing about these photographs was the fact that they were only head and shoulders. The effect was created by their expressions; here, they almost said, is part of Old England. They were known to all as 'Mr and Mrs Perriman.' They appeared, side by side, on all Perriman products. Packet soups, beef cubes, jellies, powders of every kind and variety, anything to do with food that could be put in a tin or a packet, had these pictures as trademark.

Randall was studying them when the girl surprised him by appearing again and saying: "Mr Samuel will see you now, Mr Randall."

"Oh ... thanks."

The other door was open, and Randall stepped into the great man's room.

'Great' might have been true of Samuel Perriman's reputation and position, even his ability, but it was certainly not true of his stature. He was one of nature's small men; his head and face were large in proportion to his body. He sat behind an enormous walnut desk with his back to a long, wide window. He waved a hand to an armchair.

"Sit down, Mr Randall, sit down."

"Thank you very much," said Randall. "I hope you're keeping well, Mr Perriman."

"Seldom well," said Samuel. "Indigestion. Now, Mr Randall – you have some samples, I believe. You are prepared to talk about delivery and—ah—terms. Prices. The prices quoted by your Head Office just won't do, you know, just won't do. Not competitive at all."

"I don't think we need worry *too* much about price," said Randall. He picked up his brief-case and began to open it. Samuel Perriman pressed a bell-push fitted to his desk, and the door behind Randall opened. The secretary appeared.

"Yes, Mr Samuel?"

"Bring me the Carton and Boxes sample file, please."

"Yes, Mr Samuel."

"And I feel sure you need not worry about delivery," said Randall. "We have just installed some new machinery and it has greatly increased our output. Raw materials are rather more free now, and the quality ... you won't be worried about *quality,* Mr Perriman."

Mr Samuel patted his black waistcoat.

"Quality is the basic essential of all business, Mr Randall," he announced. "Perriman's great reputation has been built up on it. *Quality Counts with Perriman's."*

He rolled off the slogan, which accompanied the pictures of 'Mr and Mrs Perriman' on all their products, and proceeded to give Randall a lecture on the sins of those companies which economised on quality.

At last the door opened and his secretary approached with a large square box, about the size of Randall's brief-case, and placed it on the desk. Randall saw that her cheeks were flushed – and he also saw a frosty glint in Mr Samuel's eyes.

"You have been a long time, Miss Morton."

"Yes, sir, I'm sorry," said Miss Morton. "The file was in Mr Akerman's room. I didn't realise he'd had it out."

"You must always know where to put your hands on these files," reproved Mr Samuel, and waved her away.

By that time Randall had taken the Crown samples from his brief-case, and was spreading them over one part of the desk. These were only dummies. They had been made up partly by hand and partly by machine, and crude drawings of 'Mr and Mrs Perriman' had been etched in black and white, together with the slogan, *Quality Counts.* When he glanced at the samples which Samuel was taking out of the file, he grimaced because they were finished productions and they looked infinitely better than his. These, undoubtedly, were samples of the small boxes and cartons which Tucktos had made for years.

Mr Samuel spread them out, lingering over each one; and they made a colourful show, for Perriman's believed in system in all things, and each product was packed in a box or packet of a different colour from the next. There were also some pages of typescript – specifications for each container.

Samuel began to talk again, earnestly, and after a while selected some of Randall's dummies. Randall did very little talking, beyond interpolating a 'yes' or 'no' or 'I understand' every few minutes. Mr Samuel bent, smoothed, and folded the dummies, sniffed them, peered at them, nodded and shook his head, put some on one pile and some on another.

Then he began to talk on a slightly higher note: "In spite of what you say, Mr Randall, I am doubtful about delivery. These custard-powder cartons, for instance – we should require …" He paused, drew in his breath as if for emphasis, and then added: "We should require a *million,* in the course of the year. A million, in equal monthly deliveries."

"Oh, we can do that," said Randall confidently.

"Very good. Price, now. You've quoted one pound eleven shillings and threepence per thousand. But it isn't competitive, Mr Randall. We shall be ordering in *millions,* as I've pointed out. Our egg powder, gravy-salt, baking-powder, dried herbs, blancmange powder, and other products are all packed in similar cartons, only the colour is different – did you understand that?"

"We quoted item by item," said Randall, and he leaned back, rubbing his hands together. "How many of that particular sized box would you require in the year?"

Mr Samuel barked: "Three million, at least!"

Randall drew a deep breath and said: "Mr Samuel, I have every confidence in your fairness, in your opinion of what is a competitive price. If you give Crown an order for three million of these boxes, colours to your specification, then Crown will be quite happy to leave the price to you."

Mr Samuel said: "Really! Have you your company's authority for saying that?"

"I think you will find that in their letter they say that I am authorised to adjust quotations," murmured Randall. "And for large quantities, I'm quite prepared to adopt the same procedure for other shapes and sizes. Write out a list of your requirements, specify your own delivery dates and prices and sign the order, Mr Perriman, and you will have no cause to regret it."

After a long pause, Mr Samuel said: "You are a very bold young man, Mr Randall."

Three-quarters of an hour later, Randall strode from the big building, his brief-case bulging, a smile that was almost fatuous on his face. He hardly noticed the corners he turned, and when he climbed into his car he let in the clutch and started the engine mechanically.

Mr Coleman's secretary was putting the black cover on her typewriter when Randall flung open the door and strode in. She stood and gaped, he was so excited. To crown her astonishment, he stepped to her side, put his arms round her shoulders and hugged her exuberantly. As he did so, Coleman came out of his office and stopped on the threshold.

"Ah'mm," he murmured.

Randall swung round, in no way abashed.

"I've got it!" he cried. "I've got it!"

Coleman said: "Got what, Mr Randall?"

"Not Perriman's order," breathed the girl.

Randall raised his brief-case in the air and gave it a resounding thwack. Because it was crammed so full, it gave out a dull, heavy sound.

"I've an order for nine million cartons, signed by the great Samuel himself, and the price is just above the minimum we were prepared to go to. I gather there's been some bother with Tucktos." Randall laughed. "Jerry Scott went in to see Samuel half-drunk and Samuel's a great temperance fanatic." With unsteady fingers he undid the straps of the brown brief-case and drew out a large envelope. "Here's the signed order – look at it! Nine million cartons! And in there I've got the key-samples we're to work from and the written specifications. A great wad of typescript, it'll take me hours to wade through it."

Coleman examined the order incredulously. It was an official form, on which 'Mr and Mrs Perriman' smiled up at all beholders; and in the bottom left-hand corner was Samuel Perriman's small, neat signature.

"I would never have believed it," Coleman breathed. "This is the biggest single order we've ever had, Randall – it's sensational. I think—I think I'll telephone the works. Mr Wilson ought to know about this immediately."

"Don't do that yet," said Randall. "I'd like to take the whole thing up to the factory in the morning. I've earned that, I think! I'll stay for an hour or two reading the specifications and making notes. I'll finish the job at my room, if needs be – and catch an early-morning train. Any objection?"

Coleman shook his head.

When it came to studying the specifications, however, Randall found that he couldn't concentrate. He kept looking at the clock in Coleman's office, and at six o'clock he telephoned to Sybil.

"Darling, I must see you for dinner!"

Sybil caught her breath.

"But, darling—"

"It's a must!" cried Randall. "Cut everything else, my precious, and meet me at Sibley's at seven o'clock. I've had the most wonderful stroke of luck!"

Louis, outside Sibley's, noticed that Miss Lennox looked over her shoulder as she approached that evening, as if she were afraid that she was being followed. And a man was walking behind her, not very far behind – the same fellow, thought Louis, who had been there at lunch-time. Miss Lennox cast a final glance over her shoulder, as the commissionaire said: "Mr Randall's inside, Miss."

"Oh." She looked startled. "Oh ... thanks."

The man who had come behind her walked past as she entered, looking straight ahead of him.

Just after half-past eight, when darkness had fallen, Randall dropped his fiancée outside her boarding-house, waited until she waved from the front door, then drove towards the corner. His head was still in the clouds. He reached the garage and put the car in.

Then he walked blithely towards Maybank. There was a street lamp at the corner. He turned the corner into the shadowy street. A lamp fifty yards farther along was shining brightly, and against it he saw a man, but he did not see the man's face. He saw a flash, a spurt of flame, heard a faint sound – and then felt as if he had been kicked violently in the chest. He reeled and dropped his case, and vaguely saw another flash.

Chapter Three

Dead Body

Guy Randall's body had been on the pavement for nearly ten minutes.

A woman's footsteps approached along the street from which he had turned. She reached the same corner, looking at the lamp which was out now – it had been broken by the murderer. She hesitated, then walked on – and saw something dark lying near the kerb. She drew to one side nervously, but as she got nearer she saw that it looked like the body of a man. He wasn't moving.

"Are you—are you ill?" she asked timidly.

The man neither moved nor answered.

Then a door opened across the road and a man called heartily: "Good night, my dear, good night!"

Light streamed out, touching the body of the man and showing a patch which glistened red on the pavement. The woman threw back her head and screamed. Across the road, the man gave a startled exclamation, and the woman with him called: "What's that?"

The woman standing by Randall's body screamed again, and the man ran across the road to her, while the woman in the doorway shouted: "Be careful, be careful!"

Another man turned the corner and a motorist swung his car into the road, its headlights revealing the whole scene and showing the bloodstains on Randall's shirt, near the V of the waistcoat. The motorist pulled up; a middle-aged woman who joined the little group looked down at the dead man, and exclaimed: "It's Mr Randall!"

She was a boarder at *Maybank*.

The man from across the road was on his knees beside the still body. He straightened up and spoke unsteadily.

"Better not touch him," he said. "Better have the police. Better 'phone."

The morgue was a low building attached to the police station, and nearly two hours after he had been discovered and pronounced dead by a doctor, Randall, stripped of his clothes, was lying on a cold, stone slab. A bright light shone above him.

The police-surgeon, Cumber, and his assistant, who were examining the body, paid little attention, at first, to anything but the two bullet wounds, one high and wide of the heart, the other through it.

A knife glinted beneath the bright light. Cumber lost himself in his work, and if he noticed the door opening, he did not look round. A big, sturdy, youthful man with close-cut dark hair and a fresh complexion walked across to the bench, and Merrick, the assistant, glanced at him. With a few deft movements, Cumber brought the two bullets nearer the surface, then motioned to Merrick, who took them out with a pair of forceps.

Cumber looked up.

"Oh, it's you, is it?"

"Hallo," said the newcomer, who was Detective-Sergeant Goodwin of New Scotland Yard. "They told me you'd got a *corpus,* so I thought I'd have a look-see."

"You'll have Adams after you," said Cumber. "He hates you Yard smarties nosing around before he's had a look himself. And he's due any time."

"I'll chance it," said Goodwin. Then suddenly his rather amused smile was wiped away. A look of alarm and incredulity replaced it, as he saw the dead man's face. He took a step forward, his hands clenched.

"Don't get worked up, it isn't West," said Cumber.

"It's uncanny," Goodwin said. "It's his double."

"Don't exaggerate," retorted Cumber. "There's a certain likeness between the dead man and Roger West, but it's superficial. Colouring, the fair, wavy hair, shape of the eyes and the upper part of the nose, but that's about all." He gave a little laugh. "I don't mind admitting that it shook me when I first saw him, and the others here were startled. We telephoned the Yard, and were told that West had been there until half-past nine and this chap was found just after nine o'clock. No need to worry."

"Of course not," said Goodwin mechanically. "He isn't so like as I thought at first glance, anyhow. But this will give West a jolt."

"Maybe," said Cumber, "but it takes a great deal to upset that young man. Well, no need to stay here. I shan't do the PM tonight," he added. "Probably tackle it first thing in the morning. Anything else you want here?"

"What do you know about him?" asked Goodwin.

"Not my show," said Cumber with a shrug. "Better see what you can find out inside. And don't forget Adams will be after your blood, he'll suspect you of trying to take a job away from him."

"Ass," said Goodwin flatly.

They left the body in the cold, bleak room, in charge of the morgue-keeper, and went into the Divisional Headquarters next door. Hardly had they arrived than Superintendent Adams, a square-shouldered block of a man, came hurrying in. He shot an unfriendly glance at Goodwin from his cold, dark-blue eyes, and then snapped out question after question. Cumber answered them patiently enough on the way to the superintendent's second-floor office. Adams went to his desk, sat down, and picked up a report.

"Want me any more?" asked Cumber.

"Eh? Oh no. 'Phone you later."

Adams nodded and said "Good night," and rang a bell. A thin man in plain clothes came in.

"What's all this, Elliott?" asked Adams.

"All in the report, sir." Elliott had a squeaky voice and a prominent nose. "Nasty business – gave us a shock; the deado looks like Mr West."

"Who?" Adams barked.

"Chief Inspector West, sir, of the Yard."

"Oh," said Adams.

"That's why I'm here," said Goodwin untruthfully.

Adams grunted and picked up the report. He read it aloud, but in exasperatingly low-pitched voice, preventing Goodwin from hearing every word.

Roger West was at home.

It was nearly midnight, and he yawned as he looked into the glowing embers of a fire which his wife, Janet, had lit because the evening had been chilly and friends had been in. West felt relaxed, pleasantly tired, and happy.

Janet came in carrying a tray; there were sandwiches as well as coffee.

"Ah, that looks good," said Roger.

"I'm glad the others wouldn't stay for some," said Janet, stifling a yawn. "I—"

The telephone bell rang.

"Oh *no*!" exclaimed Janet. "They're not going to worry you at this time of night."

Roger chuckled as he stretched out his hand to lift the receiver.

"Probably one of the guests has forgotten something," he said lightly. "Hallo."

Janet saw him frown; so it wasn't a forgetful guest. With a gesture of annoyance, she pulled up a small table and put down the tray. Then she sat back in her own arm-chair and watched Roger, who was holding on. It was now pleasantly warm in the room, which was comfortably furnished; a cheerful, modern room in a cheerful, modern house in Bell Street, Chelsea.

"Yes, speaking," Roger said at last.

A pause and then he asked: "Who? ... Oh, Goodwin. Yes?" He listened for a moment, and then said: "Well, if you really think it's urgent ... Yes, all right."

He replaced the receiver and was about to speak when Janet exclaimed: "Roger, it's too bad! Night after night you've been out. It just isn't fair – there are times when I hate your job!"

"There are certainly times when I hate it too," said Roger. "But this time—"

"That's not true. You love every minute of it. If you had to choose between giving up your job or me, it would be me every time. Don't deny it, you know it's true!"

Roger was so startled by the outburst that he looked at her in amazement. He saw the tears in her grey-green eyes. Saw the signs of strain on her face. With her dark hair falling in waves to her shoulders and looking quite at her best, Janet was lovely.

"You see, you know it's true or you'd say it wasn't," she said in a muffled voice.

Roger stood up abruptly, and knocked the table with his knee. The cups of coffee shook, coffee spilled over the edges and into the saucers.

"Oh, you fool!" exclaimed Janet.

But he steadied himself, put one arm around her, and in a moment she was pressing close to him and the tears were streaming down her cheeks. He led her to a chair, sat down, and drew her on to his lap. By that time she was groping for his handkerchief. She rubbed her eyes and blew her nose.

"I'm sorry, I didn't mean to make a fool of myself," she mumbled, "but I was hoping that you'd have a few days off, or at least not be so busy; and now Goodwin rings you up in the middle of the night and you're going off to the Yard."

"No," said Roger. "Goodwin's coming to see me and it's not official – not yet, anyhow. Nice chap, Goodwin – he's just been promoted to first-class sergeant. He's taken something so seriously that he wants to have a word with me about it, and I didn't like to turn the chap down."

"I'm not sure that this isn't worse," said Janet. "That brings the office right to our very doorstep."

Goodwin hadn't arrived when they had finished the snack, and Janet decided to go to bed. Roger went upstairs with her, and they stepped quietly into the nursery. There slept Martin called Scoopy, their elder boy. He lay on his back, breathing softly through his nose, fair hair untidy and draped over his eyes, a look of concentration on his broad, strong face. They stood looking at him a few minutes; then they went into the small spare-room, in which the second child, Richard, slept. The boys made too much noise when they were together in the nursery.

As they came out of the room and shut the door, the front door bell rang.

"I won't be long," promised Roger.

Janet squeezed his hand, and he went downstairs to let Goodwin in.

At the age of thirty, Goodwin had done very well at Scotland Yard. He had been transferred from A Division three years ago, with the rank of detective-officer, and had stepped up through third and second-class sergeant to his present first-class. After two or three years at his present rank, he was almost certain to get an early inspectorship. Roger thought he looked tired, but his eyes lighted up at the sight of the beer Janet had brought in.

Roger poured out and said: "Sit down, and tell me what's on your mind."

Goodwin sipped his beer.

"Ah, thanks. Look here, sir, have you a *brother?*"

Roger's eyebrows gave a comical lift.

"Brother? Well, yes. He—"

"In London?"

"No, he emigrated to South Africa years ago. But what's my family got to do with your worries?"

Instead of answering, Goodwin took a large envelope from beneath his coat and extracted a photograph, about 9" x 5". He handed it to Roger; obviously it had recently been printed, for it was damp to the touch. Roger turned it over, and saw Guy Randall's face. Then he saw the drool of blood-bubbly saliva at the lips, and asked sharply: "Accident case?"

"No. Murder," said Goodwin, and began to talk more freely.

Chapter Four

Danger

The case was handled at first by the Divisional staff, and the Yard was 'kept informed.' Roger followed the reports day by day. He shared an office with three other Chief Inspectors. Two of them were newly-appointed; one, who seemed to be a fixture at the Yard as well as in his rank, was Eddie Day. The room was a large, airy one, overlooking the Embankment, and was in the new building.

On the Monday morning, Roger entered the office just after ten o'clock. Eddie Day sat at his corner desk by the window, sucking his prominent, yellow teeth. Eddie's features were pointed, his nose large, and he was fat. He pretended to be reading a report. In fact, from the moment Roger entered he watched him almost furtively, muttering into his chest: "Morning, Handsome."

"Hallo, Eddie," said Roger, whose soubriquet, 'Handsome' West, was likely to stick while he remained at the Yard. "Had a good weekend?"

"So, so," said Eddie. "Got some more peas in."

"Oh, good!" said Roger absently. He sat down, stretched forward for the 'Mail In,' and saw a typewritten envelope, an internal memorandum; usually only the Assistant Commissioner sent such missives in a sealed envelope. Eddie undoubtedly knew that the note was from Chatworth, and was aching to know what it contained.

Roger slit it open, read quickly, and pulled a face.

"Anything?" Eddie demanded.

"Eh?" asked Roger, as if startled.

"Come off it," said Eddie. "Anything from Chatty? You know what I mean."

"Oh, this note. Yes, he wants to see me this morning," said Roger. "Adams isn't very happy over the Randall job. Looks as if he's going to wish it on to me."

"That Adams," grumbled Eddie. "Sits tight on a job when he ought to know better, and then expects us to get him out of a mess. If I was Chatty, I wouldn't let him get away with it so often. Why don't you refuse it?"

"I'll see what he has to say," said Roger dryly.

"Better hurry, hadn't you?" asked Eddie. "You didn't ought to keep the old boy waiting."

"He won't be ready until eleven o'clock," said Roger. "That'll give me time to look through the reports I've had in." He picked up the largest sheaf of papers in the 'Pending' tray, and began to read. From this, he learned the names of most of those people whom Guy Randall had seen on the day of his murder.

There were several pages of notes about each individual, a précis in each case of the verbatim statements which had been taken. And in all of this there were only two unusual things: first, Guy Randall's brief-case, with the Perriman order and the samples, was missing; second, the dead man's fiancée, Sybil Lennox, appeared to Adams and his men to be an unsatisfactory witness.

Had a farmer strayed into Scotland Yard, few people would have looked farther for him than the office of the Assistant Commissioner, for Sir Guy Chatworth seemed like a true man of the soil. He wore rough tweeds; his large, square face was weather-beaten, his iron-grey hair sat in little, close curls round his head, leaving a large, bald circle at the top. He smoked small, dark cheroots; he was respected by all and feared by some at Scotland Yard; and he was an able man who had the good sense to choose his subordinates carefully.

He greeted Roger gruffly in his office, which was remarkable at Scotland Yard, because – in the spacious days before austerity – he had managed to get it refurnished in a style which he liked. Only

Chatworth could have got away with black glass, chromium, tubular-steel chairs, and a general atmosphere which struck a chill into many a man who sat in front of the huge glass-topped desk and looked into Chatworth's eyes.

"Morning, Roger," he greeted. "This Randall case. The Division's got no further with it. Adams *thinks*"—he managed almost to sneer the word—"that there's something more behind it than he's been able to find out. In fact, he hasn't found much. No motive, unless it's to do with this girl Lennox – but you've kept abreast of the case, haven't you?"

"Closely, sir," said Roger.

"Go and see Adams," said Chatworth brusquely. "Take a sergeant; go through everything in detail."

"Yes, sir."

"All right, off with you," said Chatworth, but when Roger reached the door, he glanced up and asked: "Decided who you're going to take with you?"

"Goodwin," said Roger.

Chatworth grunted; it might have been with approval.

Adams' collection of written statements was verbose and voluminous, and it took Roger and Goodwin two days to wade through the lot. The routine of this was only broken by an interview with Sybil Lennox. She answered his questions frankly enough, and only showed signs of alarm when he asked her whether she had been followed on the day of Randall's murder. She denied it emphatically. Otherwise, she behaved much as Roger might have expected.

She hadn't properly recovered from the shock of Randall's death, and all the evidence pointed to the fact that she had been deeply in love with him, but she gave the impression that she was holding something back. Undoubtedly Adams had accused her of this; Roger made no mention of it then, and left her, if not happy, at least no more worried than she had been.

For the rest, he learned what the various witnesses had said; and when that was done, he went to interview them one after the other.

Thus he learned much of what Randall had done on the day of his death, and discovered that Adams had missed three things – things which he found out only after several more days of patient investigation. They were that Randall had seen Jeremiah Scott that day; that Akerman, one of the buyers at Perriman's, had heard what Scott had said; and that the proprietress of the boarding-house where Sybil Lennox lived had a poor opinion of the girl. At the end of that patient first period of investigation, exactly three weeks after Randall's death, Roger sent a chit to Sergeant Goodwin, which said briefly:

'Meet me at Sibley's at 12:45 today.'

Roger walked from the street where he had parked his car to Sibley's. He was brooding over an idea which had occurred to him the day before – a way of breaking down Sybil Lennox's resistance, or at least of finding out whether it was real or imaginary.

Louis, the commissionaire, recognised the man who walked briskly towards him, with a sense of shock.

Roger saw his intense stare and drew up by his side.

"Good morning, Louis. How are you today?"

"Haven't got over it *yet,*" declared Louis. "Just like him, you are, Inspector." Louis swallowed the last word and then gabbled: "Found-oo-did-'im-in-yet?"

"Still trying," said Roger. "The last time I saw you, you promised to think over Mr Randall's visits, especially what happened on that last day. Do you still think Randall's girlfriend was followed?"

"I'm as sure of it as I'm sure you aren't Randall," Louis declared. "I can see the fellow now, so to speak. She always walked as if the devil was on her heels, and he kept up wiv' her, although he didn't seem to hurry."

"Did she always walk like that, or only on that day?"

"Mostly always, except when she was with Randall," said Louis. "But that day she walked faster than ever. And she kept looking over her shoulder."

Roger nodded.

"He wasn't fat and 'e wasn't thin," continued Louis. "Not so tall as you and me, but not really short. Dressed in blue, and was the seat of his trousers shiny!"

"Had you ever seen him before?"

"No."

"But he was behind Miss Lennox when she came here for lunch and again when she arrived for dinner."

"I've said so, 'aven't I?"

"Yes – thanks," said Roger. "She looked scared too, I think you once said."

"S'right ... and kept looking over her shoulder."

"Had she ever looked scared before?"

Louis shook his head decidedly. "Nope."

"I see. Well, she's coming on her own this morning," said Roger. "I'm going to see her inside."

Roger went in, and was greeted by the little, old man with a thin, white beard who was Sibley.

"I have the table reserved for you, Inspector, and you won't be overheard, I've made quite sure of that."

"Thanks," said Roger. "You know it's for three?"

"Yes, it is all ready," said Sibley.

It was a corner table. Several people looked with undisguised curiosity at Roger, and at Goodwin when he came in. Goodwin's bulk seemed to fill the room.

"Hallo, sir!"

"Sit down, Jack," said Roger. "We'll wait until Miss Lennox arrives before we order drinks."

"What's the idea?" Goodwin asked.

Roger said thoughtfully: "She hasn't yet admitted that there was anything worrying her on the day of Randall's death, but the commissionaire swears that she was worried and scared of a man who followed her. I thought the atmosphere here might induce her to talk."

"I see," said Goodwin, wrinkling his forehead. "They nearly always met here, didn't they? And when she sees you again—"

"Hush!" hissed Roger.

Goodwin was well-trained, and didn't glance round. Sybil Lennox entered the room, and everyone noticed her. She looked cool. A well-cut linen frock of apple-green accentuated her figure. Her fair hair, massed in curls, was visible through the net crown of her hat. But it wasn't her dress, her figure, or her hair which caught the attention – it was her face. The lines at her eyes and the corners of her mouth heightened an impression of sadness and weariness.

Roger watched her closely.

He had already discovered that he looked even more like Guy Randall when a person looked down at him, as Sybil was looking down now. She saw him, missed a step, and clutched her bag. But it was over in a flash, and she composed herself and came forward quickly.

Roger and Goodwin stood up, a waiter pulled back a chair for Sybil, and they all sat down. The wine-waiter thrust a list in front of Roger, who said: "The Chablis, I think."

"Yes, *m'sieu*."

"If that's all right with you," Roger added, looking at Sybil.

She nodded, without speaking; her hands clenched tightly on the edge of the table. Roger had discovered that Randall and the girl had usually drunk Chablis here. If she realised that he was deliberately working on her nerves, she gave no sign but slowly relaxed. Goodwin, rather awkwardly, offered her a cigarette. Roger flicked a lighter and, when the cigarettes were alight, dropped it on to the table. Involuntarily, her gaze followed the fall of the lighter – and she drew in her breath and the cigarette fell from her lips.

The lighter was the same make as Randall's; it was a replica of the one which had been found in Randall's pocket.

She picked up her cigarette.

"Mr West," she said, "I can't understand why you want to see me again."

"I'm trying to reconstruct that last day in your late fiancé's life, Miss Lennox." Roger's voice was quiet, almost indifferent. "I'm retracing every step he took – hence this meeting." A waiter came up, with a menu for each of them, a big yellow card. "H'm ... pâté, I think."

Randall always started off with pâté.

"I'll have some thick soup," said Goodwin gruffly.

"Hors-d'oeuvre, please," said Sybil in a voice which was hardly audible. She drew deeply on her cigarette. "I can't see the point of it, Mr West? He's gone, you haven't caught his murderer, this is only … cruel."

"We're going to find his murderer," said Roger in the same quiet voice. "No matter how long it takes us, how often we have to question you, how cruel we may have to be, we're going to find out who killed him, and the first thing is to find out why he was killed. Miss Lennox, are you sure there was nothing in that brief-case which might have provided a motive?"

Chapter Five

The First Crack

Sybil didn't answer.

"After all, the brief-case was stolen," said Roger.

"He—he might have lost it."

"Oh, come!" protested Roger. "He had that huge order in the brief-case, and a single slip of paper which represented his greatest triumph. It meant everything to him, didn't it? When you were here that day, didn't he actually say to you: 'We're going places – we're in the money?'"

After a long pause Sybil said: "Yes, he did at lunch."

"That could only have been the result of his good news that day, couldn't it?" demanded Roger.

"I—I suppose so."

Roger stubbed out his cigarette. His voice altered, became sharp, decisive.

"You only suppose so. What else could it have been? In what way could he have been 'in the money' except through his work?"

She said: "Oh, it must have been that!" She seemed to have forgotten that at lunch-time Randall had not yet obtained the order.

"Are you sure?" asked Roger. "Or are you hiding something from us, Miss Lennox?"

"I—I wasn't thinking."

The waiter came up and put their plates in front of them, giving her a momentary respite. Sybil started to eat.

"Miss Lennox, I am sure you will regret it if you're not completely honest with us," Roger said.

She turned the full boldness of her gaze on him, and said deliberately: "I know of nothing else that Guy was doing to make money. Just now, I was thinking of everything that his success would have meant to us. We were so very happy."

"I simply want the truth, Miss Lennox, and must get it," Roger said gruffly. "There's another thing. When you came here on the day of Mr Randall's death, you were followed."

"I was not!"

"But I have clear evidence that you were."

She cried: "Someone's lied to you."

He didn't press the question, and the waiter brought the second course. They were half-way through it when the head-waiter came up and murmured: "You're wanted on the telephone, sir."

"Oh," Roger hesitated, then stood up, dropping his table-napkin on the table. "Thanks. Excuse me a moment," he said, and followed the head-waiter.

Immediately they were out of the room, the other man said: "I'm sorry, sir, but I thought it best to say that. Actually Louis wants to speak to you urgently."

Louis was standing in the gloomy hall, near the staircase, and as soon as Roger reached the foot of the stairs, he said hoarsely: "Come 'ere, sir – you might be seen. The chap's outside. The one that followed 'er, I mean. Come up just like 'e did before, only *she* never saw 'im. Didn't look over 'er shoulder, any'ow."

"You ought to have been a policeman," said Roger. "Go outside and keep an eye on him. I'll send a man down soon. If this merchant moves off before Miss Lennox comes out, yawn twice, where you can be seen from here."

"Oke!" Louis entered into the plot. "I'm on my way."

On the landing nearby were two telephone boxes; Roger stepped into one, and was quickly on to the Yard. He asked for Sloan.

"Bill? Roger here," he said quickly. "I want a good tailer at Sibley's pronto. Can do?"

"Yes," said Sloan.

"Good – and listen. Sybil Lennox will probably leave Sibley's in about half an hour, and be followed by a man dressed in a shiny navy-blue suit. Height about five seven."

"Want 'em both followed?"

"Yes."

"What happens if they split up?" asked Sloan.

Roger said: "Better send two men."

"I'll get cracking," promised Sloan.

Roger replaced the receiver and slipped out of the box. When he reached the dining-room, he beckoned Goodwin, who got up immediately.

"The man who followed her the other day is outside. I've sent for tailers, but they may be too late. If our man moves off, the commissionaire will look into the hall and yawn twice. You follow. If Louis doesn't signal, wait for me. Don't let the girl see you when she leaves."

"I hope the chap moves off," said Goodwin.

The girl looked up, unsmiling, as Roger returned to the table. He told her that Goodwin had to go off on another job, and over the sweet, then coffee and cigarettes, they said little.

They finished just before two o'clock. "Is there anything else?" asked Sybil. "I must get back to my office."

"I think we've said all we need say for now," said Roger.

"*I've* said everything I can," the girl assured him as she stood up. "Mr West, if you think you have to question me again, I'd be glad if you won't telephone me at my office. They will always give me a message at my rooms, but my employer is touchy about private calls while I'm at work."

"I'll avoid calling you at the office if I can," promised Roger.

She went off, and Roger smoked another cigarette. Before it was finished, Goodwin came in, looking glum. Roger grinned.

"So he waited for her?"

"Yes. Peel and Harrison are following them," said Goodwin. "I took a dekko out of the window."

"Did they go off together?"

"No. The man stood in a shop doorway, and I don't think she noticed him. He let her go half-way down the street before he followed."

"Anyone else about?" asked Roger.

"I didn't see anyone," said Goodwin. "I would have if anyone had been there."

"Jack, keep one thing in the back of your mind all the time," advised Roger. "A man was waiting round the corner for Randall, and put two bullets into his chest at point-blank range. Whoever did it was a tough customer. We've got to take every precaution. I've already arranged with old Sibley to use the back door."

He paid his bill, and they went through the kitchen quarters, where the chef, in his tall, white cap, and his satellites were relaxing after the midday rush. The head-waiter led the detectives through, and they stepped into a dingy side-street, where there were some coster's barrows piled up with fruit and several small shops. They reached Shaftesbury Avenue.

"Now what?" asked Goodwin.

"Slip along to Sibley's front entrance and make sure that no one's watching it," said Roger. "Then go back to the Yard. If I'm not in when Peel and Harrison report, follow up anything that looks urgent."

"Right-o," said Goodwin. "What are you going to do?"

"Have a word with Sybil's landlady," said Roger.

Brill Street, Chelsea, was similar to Bell Street where Roger lived only in its name. Its tall, grey, terraced houses all looked alike, except that a few had recently been painted; the tiny front gardens were mostly paved or cemented over. Some were private houses, but as Roger walked along the pavement towards number 37, where Sybil Lennox lived, he saw that almost every other front window had a notice, such as: *Bed & Breakfast; Apartments; Vacancies*. He went up the four steps leading to the front door of number 37 and rang the bell. A woman opened the door. She was middle-aged, grey-haired, sharp-featured, and wore a dark-blue dress.

"I've only one room and it's on the top floor," she announced in a flat voice.

Roger showed her his card and said: "You're Mrs Clarke, aren't you?"

"Oh, the *police*," breathed the woman. "What's it about – that Miss Lennox?"

"No," said Roger. "That Mr Randall."

"Same thing," said the landlady. "You'd better come in, I suppose." She drew to one side, and he passed into a narrow, gloomy hall. "That room there," she said, pointing, and he went into the front room which was crammed with bric-a-brac.

"I never *did* like that girl. Stuck up little brat, *and* not so particular as she might be," Mrs Clarke said with a sniff. "Too many men friends, if you ask *me*. But I'd some rooms vacant and I've got to live. She paid her rent all right, I will say that for her, but ... I never could really trust her. She must have had a good job to spend all *that* money on her clothes."

Roger nodded.

"And then there were the men," said Mrs Clarke. "Mind you, not a man stayed the *night* here – nor tried to. But I can't stop them girls seeing friends in their rooms, although out they go at ten o'clock, and they know I don't like it."

"So Miss Lennox has several men friends visiting her, does she?" asked Roger.

"She used to have."

"And you stopped it?" murmured Roger.

"I want to be honest," said Mrs Clarke self-righteously. "She stopped it herself. *And* I know why. Beneath her, she decided – she hadn't no time for the likes of them when she was in the money. The last one called about three months ago – and after that it was all Randall. Not that *he* came in here. I never set eyes on him except when he was in his car." Mrs Clarke meandered on. Rather grudgingly, she admitted that the girl had appeared to be very happy after Randall had come on the scene, following a weekend she had spent at Brighton.

It wasn't very illuminating, and Roger began to think that the visit might prove a waste of time. He would have liked to see the girl's room, but had no excuse for searching it.

He got up – and as he did so there was a thud above his head.

It made him glance up, but nothing prepared him for Mrs Clarke's sudden gasp, and her tense: "Who's that? Who is it? *It's a burglar!*"

Chapter Six

Rough-And-Tumble

"It is," she breathed. "It's a burglar!"

"It's probably one of your boarders," Roger said, moving swiftly towards the door.

"They're all out," breathed Mrs Clarke. "It's a burglar – go on, you're a policeman, catch him!"

Roger said sharply: "Listen to me; keep talking, as if I were still in the room. Whose room is above here?"

Mrs Clarke gasped: *"Hers!"*

"Keep talking," urged Roger. Mrs Clarke began to talk again, but in a low-pitched voice which didn't help at all. Roger stepped into the hall and stood close by the door. The woman's voice grew louder. Roger peered up the narrow, carpeted staircase, and started up.

He was half-way up when the door of Sybil Lennox's room opened an inch; he saw bright daylight coming through. Whoever was in the room could see the bottom of the staircase and the hall-passage, but not the landing. Roger reached the landing and stepped close to the wall. The door opened wider. He saw the shadow of a man on the floor and the wall opposite.

The man stepped out of the room, and went to the wooden rail and peered over the stairs. He was short and rather plump – he wore the kind of hat Louis had talked about. He carried a brief-case in his right hand; his breathing was wheezy and sounded plainly. Roger took a step forward. The floor was covered with linoleum, which gave a slight squeak under his foot.

The man swung round.

He raised the brief-case and struck at Roger's head.

The corner caught Roger in the eye, a shoot of pain darted across his head, water welled up, blinding him – and the next moment his assailant kicked him in the stomach. The ferocity of the attack made Roger back to the wall, unable to see, bending forward slightly because of the pain in his stomach. He felt himself grabbed by the shoulder and pushed away; in spite of the pain he sensed that the man was rushing towards the head of the stairs, and he stuck out his leg.

The man fell over it, and crashed down, making the landing and the passage shake. Mrs Clarke gave a high-pitched scream which echoed through the house. The man swore, and Roger heard him scrambling to his feet and, through the tears in his uninjured eye, saw him vaguely. Roger jumped forward, striking out blindly and wildly. He caught the man's face and brought a grunt. Another blow missed; the man grabbed his wrist, twisted, and thrust him backwards. As he fell, he heard Mrs Clarke still screaming, heard footsteps thudding on the stairs. So he'd lost his man. He came up against the wall, banging his head painfully, making his eyes water more freely.

Then he heard a man say: "Oh, no, you don't!"

That was Goodwin's voice.

"*He's got a gun!*" screeched Mrs Clarke.

"Don't be a fool!" said Goodwin in a harsh voice. "If you use that, you're for the high jump."

Then – *crack!*

The report rang out, and Roger saw the flash of the shot through the mist of tears. He glimpsed Goodwin reeling down the stairs and the man following him. Goodwin hit the wall with a thud and fell. The man jumped over him.

Roger gripped the handrail and leapt over. The gunman looked round and saw him. Roger landed on a stair just above Goodwin's inert body. He slipped, staggered backwards and then fell on to

Goodwin. Mrs Clarke had disappeared, a door closed like a thunderclap, and the gunman was touching the front door-knob with his left hand and looking behind him. His gun pointed at Roger.

Crack!

The bullet smacked into the wood of the banisters, splintering it. As he regained his feet, Roger snatched his cigarette-case out of his pocket and flung it – he had no other missile. The man ducked and fired again.

This time the bullet hit the wall.

Roger was in the passage now, but the front door was open. The man jumped down the street steps.

Roger reached the porch and saw the fellow running towards the Embankment; then another mist of tears smeared his vision. He shouted: "Police! Police!"

Another dark figure appeared from a doorway, and ran in the same direction as the gunman. Roger could suddenly see more clearly, the spasm of pain and tears had eased. He saw the gunman turn and fire; he missed, but forced the pursuer to lose pace. He reached the corner and disappeared – and as he did so, a car pulled up alongside Roger.

A man said: "What's the trouble?"

"End of the road – turn left!" snapped Roger. He sprang on to the running-board of the car and clasped the door handle. The wind cut into his eyes, and he lowered his head and with his free hand wiped the tears away. The traffic passing along the Embankment seemed to move very fast, but as they drew up there was a gap, and the driver was able to swing left without halting.

The gunman was on the pavement, opposite the riverside, threading his way among startled people. As he went, he looked over his shoulder and saw Roger clinging to the car.

He darted into the road.

Whether he hoped to double-back or did that just to un-sight Roger, Roger never knew.

The man disappeared from his line of vision, but almost at once brakes squealed. He heard a woman scream again, then heard a thud.

The driver of the commandeered car gasped: "Oh, my God!"

His hands slackened on the wheel, the car wobbled, then he regained control, coming to a standstill fifty or sixty yards from the end of Brill Street. Looking past him through the far window, Roger saw a car with its rear wheels on the pavement, its front wheels turned towards him – and a shattered hulk of what had been a man lying in the roadway.

The law went into action. Three policemen appeared and took charge of the crowd, the body, the car, and its injured driver – not badly injured, but cut about the hands and face. Roger spoke to a sergeant of the uniformed branch, giving instructions for the body to be taken to Cannon Row morgue, and men to be sent to 37 Brill Street.

He went back himself, and found that a small crowd had gathered outside and the little passage was packed with people. Two policemen, a man in dark-brown, Mrs Clarke, two other women – and Goodwin still on the stairs. Roger pushed his way through, and recognised the man in brown as Sergeant Peel, one of the men who had been sent from the Yard to follow Sybil and her 'companion.'

"Hallo, sir," said Peel quietly. "Afraid Goodwin's in a bad way."

"Not dead?" Roger rasped.

"No, sir, but I've sent for an ambulance and a doctor. Should be here any minute. Best to leave him where he is, I think. He's got a bullet in the chest, about where Randall got it. I've padded it, to stop the bleeding." Peel's short sentences were graphic, indicating his frame of mind. "He's unconscious, doesn't feel anything. Did the swine get away?"

"He ran into a car."

"Dead?" exclaimed Peel.

Roger nodded and heard a bell ringing, the ambulance turning into Brill Street. It had hardly drawn up outside before a car followed, and the Divisional Police Surgeon stepped out. He made a brief examination of the injured man and said: "An operation might save him."

The ambulance men came in with a stretcher. Roger watched them carry Goodwin out.

"Station a man outside and send another to the back of the house until we've finished here," he said to Peel. "Get the name and address of the driver of the car I used, and get rid of him nicely. Then come upstairs to me. Don't let Mrs Clarke leave the house, and if any of the boarders turn up, they're to wait down here until I give the all-clear."

"Right, sir," said Peel.

Roger went slowly up the stairs and into the girl's room. It was large, bright and airy, and the furniture was modern. He glanced at his face in the mirror; there was a dark bruise just above his right eye, where the brief-case had caught him.

The brief-case ...

He reached the door as Peel stepped on to the landing.

"Have you seen a light-brown brief-case, Peel?"

"One was found downstairs, sir," said Peel. "I had it wrapped in brown paper, and it's now on the hall-stand. Shall I go and get it?"

"Please," said Roger.

He sat down on the edge of the bed and rubbed his stomach, which was sore from the kick. Peel brought in the brown-paper parcel and a cup of tea.

"Thought you might be glad of this," he said. "Like a spot of whisky in it?"

"Not a bad idea!"

Roger felt brisk and clear-headed when he put the cup and saucer on the mantelpiece, and talked to Peel. The sergeant's story was simple enough. He had followed the man from the restaurant, and Sergeant Harrison had followed the girl, who had returned to her office in the Strand. Harrison was still there and would follow her tonight. The unknown man had come to Chelsea, and Peel had seen him enter the tiny back garden of number 37. By chance, a radio-patrol car had been passing, and he had asked the driver to send a message to Goodwin, who had hurried here. Peel had spoken to him, and then Goodwin had come round to watch the front while Peel had watched the back.

Goodwin, presumably had found the door open – or Mrs Clarke had let him in – and entered the house when he had heard the noise. Peel had heard the shooting, and rushed along an alley which led from the back of the houses to the street. He had arrived just as Roger had commandeered the car.

"Let me have a look at that brief-case," said Roger. "Anyone but you handled it?"

"No, and I used a handkerchief."

"Good." Roger pulled on a pair of thin, blue cotton gloves, picked up the case by the handle and then unfastened the straps, careful not to touch the shiny surface of the leather more than he could help. He soon had the case open and turned back the flap.

Written in neat, black writing was Randall's name and address.

Chapter Seven

A Man Named Kirby

Peel's eyes glistened.

"So we've got it," he observed. "No doubt that devil had something to do with Randall's death. Probably his killer – he fired point-blank at Goodwin – aimed at the chest, and the gun was a small one."

"You saw it?" asked Roger.

"Just caught a glimpse of it in his hand," said Peel. "And I heard it – sounded like the whine of an automatic to me; it wasn't a revolver, anyhow."

"The man had the case in his hand after he'd dealt with me," said Roger. "He dropped it by accident when he fell over Goodwin. The question is, did he come to get it from here or did he come to plant it on Sybil Lennox?"

Peel said slowly: "If he'd come to plant it, would he have troubled to take it away again?"

"Might have," said Roger. "It would have been one thing to leave it here without anyone knowing he'd been in the house, another to leave it when he'd been seen and it might be guessed that he'd brought it here. If recent prints of Sybil Lennox are on it, then the case has probably been here all the time. We'll get a sample of her prints," he added, looking at the dressing-table. "Got your kit with you?"

"Afraid not, sir."

"Mine's in my car, parked along the street," said Roger. "Get it, will you? I'll look round."

Against the wall, opposite the large single bed, was a big wardrobe; in a corner there was another smaller one. A tallboy with eight drawers stood near the bed, and the dressing-table backed on the window.

There were no letters or papers in any of the drawers. He tried the wardrobes. Sybil Lennox had plenty of clothes, and all seemed expensive; he could more easily understand Mrs Clarke's gossip. Unless Sybil was earning a very high salary, she hadn't bought these out of her ordinary income.

Peel came in with the case of equipment, and while Roger looked through the drawers at the foot of the tall wardrobe, Peel brushed some of the grey powder over a powder-bowl and a hairbrush handle, and then blew it gently away.

"Good prints?" asked Roger.

"Perfect."

"Photograph 'em," said Roger briefly. He knew that Peel would have a Leica with him and was an enthusiast. The camera clicked, and by then Roger had practically finished his search of the room. Nothing of interest was found.

"Lend me a hand with the mattress," he said.

Peel went to the other side of the bed and they rolled back the mattress, bedclothes, and all. They didn't have to look any farther, for under the mattress there were some colourful pieces of cardboard, and from several of them two familiar faces peered out – the faces of 'Mr and Mrs Perriman.'

"So we've got his samples," breathed Peel. "And that means we've got her!"

Sybil Lennox worked in the drawing-office of a small firm of architects and surveyors, the firm of Boyd & Fairweather. Boyd was seldom in the office, but Fairweather was usually there, a small, grey, bespectacled man with a shrill voice and a quick temper.

She was not back in the office until nearly twenty minutes to three that afternoon, but he made no comment on her late return from lunch.

Just after four o'clock, the telephone rang; it was for her. She asked in a husky, rather nervous voice: "Who is that?"

She held the receiver tightly; she seemed to sway; she did more listening than talking, and her voice was hardly audible when she said at last: "All right, goodbye."

Detective-Sergeant Harrison stood near the entrance to a block of offices in which the firm of Boyd & Fairweather was housed, contemplating some aeroplane, steamship, and motor-car models in a toy shop. He saw everyone who entered the office block with a photographic eye, for although others seldom registered him in their minds, everyone registered in his.

It was nearly five o'clock.

Traffic in the Strand was never slack during the day, but during the last ten minutes the crowds, the cars, taxis, and buses had become thicker as rush-hour approached, and there were several hold-ups. People pushed past Harrison. In his mind's eye he had a picture of Sybil Lennox. A taxi drew up nearly opposite the exit. Harrison simply noticed the fact and also noticed the driver. He had some sticking-plaster over his face and forehead and his right hand was heavily bandaged. He had a rather long nose, with a piece of sticking-plaster attached to the bridge. The tip of the nose was sore, and his right eye was half closed by a bruise.

Harrison walked past him, and therefore past the entrance to the building, so as to get a closer look at the man who lit a cigarette as Harrison passed, and lowered his face towards his cupped hands.

Harrison turned and walked back to his original position. The girl was standing just inside the building. On her face was an expression of rapt attention – she was staring into the Strand, *at the taxi-driver*. Harrison caught on in a flash; she was waiting for the driver to signal her to come forward!

The plain-clothes man showed no sign that he understood this, but looked into a window where some hand-made boots and shoes were displayed. There was a traffic block stretching from Trafalgar Square; the lights were against the stream. Soon the traffic began to move, and the driver with the bandages tossed his cigarette out of the window. The girl came out, hurrying.

Harrison glanced eagerly at the line of traffic for a taxi with its flag up; there wasn't one, there wouldn't be one at this hour. He noted the number and make and colour of the cab. There was a public telephone in a confectioner's shop nearby; he swung round towards the shop, and almost fell over a little man who staggered away from him.

"Sorry," muttered Harrison.

"I should ruddy well think you are sorry!" screeched the little man fiercely. He was almost a dwarf, and barely came up to Harrison's chest. His thin face was suffused with rage, and he hopped about on one foot like a man possessed. "Nearly broke my ankle, you great clodhopper."

"Sorry," repeated Harrison. "I didn't mean—"

"Ought to look where you're going, you clumsy basket," screeched the little man. A crowd had swiftly collected; men, women, boys, and girls paused in their homeward rush.

"I've said I'm sorry. You're not badly hurt. Don't crowd round, please."

The crowd pressed closer, the policeman's voice without a uniform was ineffective. The words had incensed the little man even more too; he wanted his assailant's name and address. Harrison pushed past him and tried to break through the crowd, but it was too thick.

The little 'victim' swung his injured leg at him and caught him a terrific blow on the ankle with the toe of his boot. Harrison was suddenly engulfed in pain which ran from his ankle to the rest of his body like a burning flame. He staggered and lost his footing.

It was nearly twenty minutes after Sybil Lennox had entered the taxi before Harrison got his message through to the Information Room.

About the time that the girl appeared at the doorway, Roger West reached Scotland Yard with Peel. He sent Peel along to the Fingerprints Room with the brief-case, his photographs, and the coloured specimens of Perriman's boxes, all to be tested for prints. He went to his own office, and was glad to find it empty. He picked up the telephone receiver.

"Put me through to the Cheyne Hospital, please," he said and held on. In the 'Mail In' partition was a small automatic pistol with the handle badly scratched, and with a label tied to it; on the gun were traces of finger-print powder. Also tied to it was a live cartridge – presumably the only one found in the magazine of the gun. It was, of course, the gun which had been used that afternoon. The label which Roger read when he pulled it towards him ran:

Walton -22 automatic pistol, found near body of man believed to be Arthur Kirby at scene of accident on Chelsea Embankment, March … at 3:34pm.

The smaller label tied to the bullet read:

Walton -22 automatic pistol bullet taken from gun found near body of Arthur Kirby. See gun.

"You're through, sir," said the operator.

"Thanks. Cheyne Hospital? … This is Scotland Yard. A Sergeant Goodwin was brought in this afternoon with a bullet wound in his chest, can you tell me how he is, please? … Yes, I'll hold on."

He heard footsteps outside and saw the door-handle turn. Eddie Day's nose and stomach preceded their owner into the room.

"Why, hallo 'Andsome! They tell me—"

"Hush!"

Eddie tip-toed towards Roger as the woman at the hospital spoke again.

"The bullet has been removed and the patient is as comfortable as can be expected," she said.

"Is he on the danger-list?"

"Oh yes. I'm afraid he will be for some time. Am I speaking to a friend of the patient?"

"Yes."

"I think his relatives should be summoned as quickly as possible," said the woman.

"I'll see to it, thank you," said Roger gruffly.

He replaced the receiver and stared up into Eddie's face.

"Goodwin in a bad way, 'Andsome?"

"Very. He lives in the Marylebone Road. I think I'll go and see his wife myself."

"Anything I can do while you're gone?" asked Eddie.

"Tell Peel I'll be back by half-past five," said Roger, "and tell him we'll be working late tonight. He'll take Goodwin's place."

"Right-o, 'Andsome."

Roger went downstairs. His car was parked near the front entrance, but as he started the engine, a tubby little man wearing a tweed suit came hurrying across the yard.

"Oi—Handsome!"

Roger looked at him unsmilingly.

"See the Back-room Inspector," he said. "I've got nothing for you just now, Tommy."

"Oh, come off it," said the plump little man. "The *Echo's* always first – remember the old tag. Just a sentence, that's all I want."

"As soon as I can, but not now," said Roger.

He drove as quickly as the traffic would permit to Goodwin's home.

Chapter Eight

New Aspect

Goodwin lived in a flat above a newsagent's shop at the Edgware Road end of Marylebone Road. There was a side door and a narrow passage. The door was ajar, and Roger pushed it open and stepped inside. The first thing he saw was a pram, and he had to squeeze past it to reach the narrow stairs. Goodwin had one child, a girl of nearly two – only the day before Goodwin had been saying that she was getting too big for her pram. Half-way up the stairs, he heard a woman laugh and a child chuckle.

The door at the head of the stairs was closed. Roger tapped on the small, iron knocker, and the woman's voice stopped but the child's gurgles continued.

"Now be quiet, Marjorie, Mummy's got to go to the door. Stay there, mind."

Footsteps followed, and Roger ran his fingers through his hair and wiped his forehead. He had met Mrs Goodwin only twice. She was a small, round-faced woman with mischievous, blue eyes and a well-developed, almost dumpy figure. She was half-smiling when she opened the door. Recognition came swiftly, and with it understanding, at least, that he brought bad news. The smile vanished.

"What is it, Mr West? Is he hurt?"

"I'm afraid so," said Roger, stepping past her into the living-room of the flat. "He's been shot, Mrs Goodwin. They've got the bullets out and are doing everything they can. But I think you ought to know that he's on the danger-list."

"Where is he?"

"Cheyne Hospital, in Chelsea."

"How soon can I get there?"

"I'll take you. I've got the car downstairs," said Roger. Mrs Goodwin didn't answer at once, but looked round at her daughter.

"I'll have to take her," she said. "We don't know anyone well enough here to leave her with. I won't be five minutes."

She wasn't. Soon she and Marjorie climbed into the back of the car, and Roger started off. Neither adult spoke, and the child kept quiet, as if the visitation had depressed her too. Roger went the long way round, to keep clear of traffic. Suddenly he said: "Mrs Goodwin, my wife will look after Marjorie for a few hours. We live near the hospital."

"Oh, I can't give her such trouble!"

"Don't worry about that, and she'll be quite happy with our two boys. I think we ought to drop Marjorie first," Roger went on. "It won't make five minutes difference."

Scoopy and Richard, wearing bright red sun-suits, were playing in the back garden and came rushing into the front when they heard the car. Janet was upstairs; Roger saw her at the window as he climbed out. He beckoned her, and by the time the two boys and Marjorie had been introduced, Janet had appeared at the front door.

"What is it, Roger?"

Before he had finished telling her, she was on her way to the car. It was quickly arranged that Mrs Goodwin should return to Bell Street when she had to leave the hospital. Within five minutes, Roger was driving off again. When they reached the hospital he was relieved to see Bill Sloan in the big, austere, white-walled hall, and Sloan immediately had a word of cheer.

"No sign of a relapse, they tell me. Are you going up with Mrs Goodwin?"

"Can you?" asked Roger. "I ought to get back."

"Gladly. Come on, Nell," said Sloan, and Roger realised for the first time that Sloan and the Goodwins were friends. Nell Goodwin turned to Roger, started to speak but couldn't, and hurried along with Sloan. Roger didn't wait, but walked back to his car.

When he arrived at the Yard he hurried along to his office. Peel was waiting by himself. Roger looked at several packets and articles on his desk – the gun, and two more bullets, each with a label attached.

"Got the ballistics people busy already?" he asked.

"Yes," said Peel, "but there's something else."

"Let's have it."

Peel told him what had happened to Harrison, and also that the taxi-cab had not been traced. Its number was not registered at Scotland Yard as a licensed ply-for-hire vehicle, which meant that it either had false number-plates or was used without a licence.

"Have you put a call out for Sybil Lennox?" Roger asked.

"Yes."

"Good. And is Harrison's description of the taxi-driver good enough to send round?"

"Yes, I've sent it," said Peel. "Harrison's up in the rest-room, with his leg stretched out, writing a report … oughtn't you to see him?"

"Right away," said Roger.

Harrison's right foot was heavily bandaged. He was bending over a table, twisted round awkwardly, and writing furiously when the others arrived. He immediately apologised for making a mess of the job.

"No one's fault," said Roger briefly. "I'm worried about this little man who made the scene. Any doubt that he did it deliberately?"

"None."

"This cabby – what did he look like?"

"As a matter of fact, he'd been in the wars, obviously had an accident quite recently," said Harrison. "That's why I took so much notice of him and was able to send the description round. I did wonder whether the plaster and the bandages were a blind, to make identification difficult, but I seem to remember that he had a little raw patch on the tip of his nose."

"Just a minute," said Roger sharply and spun round. "Peel, get on to Chelsea. Ask them for a detailed report on the injuries to the driver of the car which ran over Kirby. It looked as if Kirby had an accident, but it's just possible that he was deliberately run down. If he knew the car was waiting for him on the Embankment, he'd try to reach it, and if the driver thought that he was in serious trouble, he might have driven at him."

The driver of the car which had killed Kirby had given his name as Smith and submitted a driving licence in that name. But before eight o'clock that night, it was discovered that the driving licence belonged to another man, who had lost it some weeks before and who, during that afternoon, had been on the other side of London. The smashed car had been hired, also by a 'Mr Smith,' from a drive-yourself hire company in the West End, and a deposit had been paid in old pound notes. 'Smith' himself had been patched up by a local doctor, and had refused to be taken home in a police-car but insisted on taking a taxi.

There was a call out for the taxi-driver who had picked him up, and the man reported at Bow Street Police-Station at half-past eight. He had dropped his passenger near Long Acre.

All this, Roger discovered while sitting at his desk. The lights in the office were on, and Peel was sitting at Eddie Day's desk, drawing up a report. There had been no response to the call for the pseudo-taxi-man, the little man, or Sybil Lennox. There was some information about Kirby. He had lived in a rooming-house near New Oxford Street for the past six weeks, renting a furnished room and getting all his own food; no one there knew much about him. He seldom had visitors, and the only one whom the proprietor of the house remembered clearly was a woman named Rose, aged about thirty.

Even without the attack on Goodwin, the Yard and the Divisions would have been keyed up to a high pitch, but the fact that Goodwin might die added a touch of fervour to their activities. Chatworth telephoned from his flat in Victoria, to inquire after Goodwin, and told Roger that he could have a free hand. That was at half-past nine.

Roger stretched himself as he replaced the receiver.

"Better have a snack, hadn't we?" said Peel.

"Go and get us something from the canteen, will you?" asked Roger, and Peel went at once.

Roger picked up a pencil and began to doodle. He let his thoughts roam freely; the case had to be viewed from a new angle. Before, it had been regarded as a 'domestic crime;' but Kirby, the little near-dwarf, and the taxi-driver obviously belonged to the same group. They were no longer looking for one individual, but for forces behind the individual. In short, they were up against an organisation.

Was the girl a party to Randall's murder? Did she play a part in some undiscovered racket? Had she struck up an acquaintance with Randall on someone else's instructions in an effort to use Randall? If so, there might be reason for thinking that the murder had something to do with Randall's business or his travels.

The telephone bell rang and Roger lifted the receiver.

"West."

"It's me, darling," said Janet quietly; she sounded very subdued.

"Oh, my sweet, I'm so sorry. I quite meant to call you and—"

"I guessed you wouldn't be home early," said Janet. "Mrs Goodwin's staying here for the night. I've put the two boys together and Marjorie in Richard's room. Mrs Goodwin's going to have your bed. I'll put the camp-bed up in the dining-room for you."

Roger said: "Bless you."

"Oh, and Mark's here," added Janet. "He's just called out, are you likely to be in before midnight?"

"I doubt it," said Roger. "Remind him he's an ordinary civilian, will you, and should stick to his china and textbooks. Sweet, I must go."

"Take care of yourself," Janet said, with a catch in her voice.

As Roger replaced the receiver, Peel came in with some beef sandwiches, cheese rolls, and tea. Roger munched and drank. Peel took two further negative reports about the search for the woman named Rose, and Roger started thinking about the case again. That taxi-driver, for instance …

He started up and nearly choked.

"Gone down the wrong way," asked Peel, sympathetically.

Roger took a swig of tea.

"The man who called himself Smith. He was dropped near Long Acre. There are several taxi-garages just at the back of Long Acre. Smith left Chelsea, went straight to Long Acre, and was outside the Strand office in the taxi within an hour. So he must have got his cab very quickly."

Peel grabbed a telephone. "The Squad?"

"Yes – and Divisions, for a cordon round that area," ordered Roger.

Chapter Nine

Taxi

It was very dark and still hot – oppressively hot, as if a storm were brewing. In the back streets near Long Acre there was little noise after eleven o'clock. Now and again a cab drove into a garage, and when the driver left he was stopped and questioned by the police. Every one of the thirty detectives who were concentrated on this small area of London knew that they were looking for a 1928 Morris cab with a bull-nose, the body painted dark-blue, the wings and chassis black. They had a description of the little man who had delayed the observant Harrison and photographs of Kirby. The cab wasn't in any of the five garages in the vicinity, so it might be driven in at any time.

Roger was at the corner of a narrow road, opposite a small garage. Peel wasn't far away, near one of the larger garages. A few night-birds walked past. It seemed to get hotter, and in the distance there was a rumble of thunder and a dim flash; a storm was on its way. Roger eased his damp collar and thought he felt a spot of rain. He hadn't brought a coat – there wasn't a mackintosh among the whole party. A light from the garage shone on a girl – or someone who at first looked like a girl. She walked past quickly, and the light shone on her hennaed hair, her garishly made-up face, the flimsy dress stretched tight over her full figure.

A cabby coming out of the garage called: "Hallo, dearie!"

"Be yourself," said the 'girl,' but she was in the middle thirties, Roger thought.

The woman passed, the cabby came across the road, and Roger and the detective-officer near him stepped forward. The cabby started.

"What's this?"

"Let's have a look at you," said Roger. "Turn round, will you?" He looked into a burly face and smelt beer, then showed his card. "Where have you been today?"

"Usual. Central."

"Do you know a man named Kirby?"

"Never 'eard of him."

"Another driver named Smith?"

The man guffawed. "Dozens, I should say!" He took out a packet of cigarettes. "What's up?"

"Murder," said Roger, and the man frowned. "You spoke to a girl just now. Do you know her?"

"Seen her about sometimes," said the cabby. "She comes to meet her boyfriend, I s'pect. Some of them do."

"Do you know her name?"

"No, *and* I don't want to. I ..." He stopped and scratched his stubble. "Come to think, I do. I went over to Harry Wignall's to borrow a bit of light-cable, coupla nights ago, and she met her boyfriend. I heard him say: 'Hallo Rosie!'"

"Rosie, was it? What was her boyfriend like?" demanded Roger. "Is he a cabby?"

"'E 'ad a badge on," said the cabby, touching his own enamel disc with his number on it.

"Have a look at this," said Roger, and shone a torch on to a photograph of Kirby, taken after death and touched up. The cabby took it, and conceded that it might be the man. Roger described the near-dwarf who had attacked Harrison; short, pale, bald-headed, and with a pointed nose and receding chin.

"Oh, I know *Relf*," said the cabby. "He's at ..."

He broke off.

"I said this was murder," said Roger roughly.

"You there, sir?" Peel's voice came softly as he approached the corner. "I think we've found—" He stopped when he saw the cabby. "Sorry."

"It's all right. Who've you found?"

"The girl Rose, I think," said Peel. "I haven't tackled her yet, thought I'd leave it to you, but her name's Rose and she comes here regularly to meet a driver named Kirby. Kirby's got his own cab, and keeps it at Wignall's garage."

Roger turned to the taxi-driver.

"Does this man Relf work at Wignall's?"

"Supposing 'e does?"

Roger said sharply: "You're asking for trouble." He turned away with Peel. "Did this Rose go into Wignall's garage?"

"Yes. We'll stop her if she comes out."

They walked along the road as spots of rain fell. The rumbling of thunder sounded nearer, and by the time they reached Wignall's garage, it was raining hard; Roger turned up his jacket collar.

The garage was the largest he had seen here. Already two or three dozen cabs were in, showing up eerily in the dim, yellow light from naked electric light bulbs. The only bright light was in a corner, where a partition had been erected, wood at the bottom and glass at the top. On the glass was printed in black the word: *Office*.

The office was tiny, and a bald-headed man sat at a high desk, looking at 'Rose.' She was sitting on a high stool and swinging her legs; by her side was a bottle of beer and a mug, and a cigarette dangled from her lip. The man stared at her intently. He had a long pointed nose and a very little chin, which seemed to have been driven into his neck.

Peel muttered: "That's Harrison's assailant!"

"Looks like it," said Roger.

Outside, the rain pattered down and a clap of thunder sounded very loud. The man and the girl glanced towards the door and the two detectives made clear silhouettes against a flash of lightning which lit up the street behind them. For a split second the man sitting at the desk seemed transfixed. Then in a flash he was off his stool – and he stood only a head above the desk.

The girl exclaimed: "What's biting you?"

The man pushed her off the stool towards the doorway, and for the first time Roger saw another door, leading out of the office.

The girl shouted as she toppled over. The bottle of beer fell on to the floor, the mug followed and smashed into dozens of pieces. As the noise of the smash came, Roger put a whistle to his lips – but the shrill blast was drowned in another loud clap of thunder. The door of the office opened and the dwarf disappeared.

Roger blew again, and this time the blast was deafening. The girl hadn't yet started to pick herself up, but was shaking her right hand, which was bleeding. Roger reached her a yard in front of Peel, put his hand on the desk inside the office and leapt over her. He went through the open doorway and saw a flight of wooden steps. Now he could hear a man walking above his head.

Peel was close behind him.

He wished that he had brought a gun, and Chatworth would have given him authority; but that couldn't be helped now. He reached the top of the stairs and found himself in a huge, dimly lighted loft. Only part of the loft was boarded over to make a floor, and on it were piled tyres and boxes of tubes and other accessories.

The little man, Relf, was behind a stack of tyres. He had something in his hand, and hurled it at Roger – it was a tyre-lever, which crashed on a rafter, aimed much too high, but as it fell the end struck Roger lightly on the shoulder. He stooped to pick it up – it was better than no weapon at all.

Relf disappeared again. Peel was just behind Roger.

"Shout down that he's up here," ordered Roger. "Let's have some more men up, but watch the street and the roof. We—"

A thunderclap burst out immediately above their heads, and a vivid flash came through two small windows. The only light when the flash was over came from the dim bulbs downstairs and on the staircase. Roger crept forward cautiously, clutching the tyre-lever.

Then he caught a glimpse of Relf, slipping from one pile of tyres to another.

Near Roger's hand was a rack in which were dozens of loose sparking-plugs. He slipped half a dozen into his pocket, took one in his hand – and the next time Relf appeared he hurled the plug. It struck a tyre and bounced off. Relf was getting close to one of the windows and also near the end of the flooring. He seemed to have no other weapon.

Roger was now no more than ten yards away from him, with another sparking-plug raised. He saw a shadow on the wall, a large, vague shape, cast by a lamp below. The brief quiet was uncanny. Several of his men were now upstairs, others were probably on the stairs, and more in the garage and in the adjacent street, but everywhere was still – except for the pattering of the rain.

Then something flashed across his eyes, and he darted back. A knife stuck quivering in a wooden upright close by his side. It hadn't come from Relf, but from the other direction; there must be two men up here.

A clap of thunder roared and reverberated, a man gave a high-pitched, unnatural scream, tyre-levers hurtled towards the police; and the shadow moved.

It was Relf's shadow right enough – Relf was now close to the window, glancing behind him. The man on the other side of the loft was hurling everything he could lay his hands on at Roger and those police who were approaching Relf. To reach the little man, Roger would have to pass through that barrage.

He ducked and scudded across the loft, with tyre-levers and spanners hurtling above his head. He heard a thud and a gasp as one of his men was hit. Something brushed across his head and he felt a stinging sensation in his scalp. All this, while Relf opened the window and, being small, squeezed through without difficulty.

He slammed the window behind him.

Roger swung the tyre-lever and smashed the glass. He glanced to his left, where Peel and three other Yard men were advancing on Relf's ally. The man was defenceless and backing towards the wall. He was uttering an unintelligible gibberish in a reedy, horrible voice.

But he'd helped Relf to get away.

Another man joined Roger as he thrust a piece of steel between the window and the frame and levered sharply. The hinges broke and the window leaned drunkenly to one side; there was hardly room to get through. A flash of lightning lit up the whole sky. In a fantastic second, a hundred things were shown in that vivid light. Chimneys of all shapes and sizes, roof-tops, glinting windows, the scintillating rain.

And it revealed Relf.

A fire-escape, just an iron ladder, sloped upwards from the window to the roof of the next building. Beneath was a drop of forty or fifty feet. The little man was crouching on the other roof and looking towards Roger. He moved as the lightning faded – but hardly had the darkness fallen than a detective behind Roger directed a powerful torch on the man. Relf was getting behind a chimney-stack.

"Shall I go, sir?" asked Roger's companion.

"No," said Roger. "Take this."

He gave the man the tyre-lever, and hauled himself through the window. He gripped the sides of the ladder, finding it slippery with the rain, which soaked him in an instant. It was only ten feet up to the next building, but if Relf had a gun ...

"Keep me covered," he muttered.

"What's that, sir?"

Roger didn't speak again; in any case, a rumble of thunder followed and the rain splashed down with greater violence. Roger crawled up the ladder, and was half-way when a lightning flash revealed Relf standing behind the chimney-stack *with a gun in his hand.*

So this was it.

Roger saw the flash, heard the report, and felt the ladder quiver, but no pain. Then darkness again – and the man behind him switched off his light. All was safe until the next flash of lightning, but he daren't hurry; if he hurried he would slip.

He let himself go forward, then eased himself up the sloping roof until he touched the rough-cast of the chimney-stack. He was able to grip the chimney, and drew himself up to his full height.

A torch beam shone out, striking the roof not far away; others came on quickly. Only a few were behind Roger; others came from men standing on the roofs across the road. Windows were lit up, some bright, some little more than dim, yellow squares. One powerful light was coming from a window some way off; there was searchlight power in its brightness, and it showed the whole of the roof on which Roger was standing – a fifty or sixty yard expanse broken only by chimney-stacks. The slope from the guttering on either side was gentle; it would be possible to walk safely but for the streaming rain which ran and gurgled over the slates. Through the silvery streaks he could see men standing on other roofs – and saw Relf, when lightning flashed.

Relf was crouching only two stacks away from him.

Roger began to move forward. A man shouted: "Wait, sir, wait; don't let him get you."

Some sense in that – but caution wasn't good enough. Relf might kill himself; and he had to be caught alive. Roger crept forward. The roof wasn't as slippery as he had feared. Lightning came again, and the thunder which followed was farther away. The rain was easing a little.

He caught another glimpse of Relf, near the far end of the roof; he seemed to be looking for a way of getting across to the next block. He looked round at Roger and fired.

Roger didn't know where the bullet struck; he heard nothing. He reached the next stack, the last one between him and Relf, and crouched out of danger. Peering round, he could just see the little man. Although not bright, the light was good enough. Touch and go now. If Roger left his chimney-stack, Relf would have him at point-blank range; if he didn't, Relf would have time to find the ladder which connected this roof to the next. It looked as if he'd found it. He bent forward and touched something, then looked round again. Roger dodged back, out of sight. This hide-and-seek could go on for a long time; they wanted someone on the next roof, and – two men appeared there.

So it was nearly over. Relf couldn't go forward and couldn't come back. He had seen the two detectives, who wore hats and raincoats; Relf was standing upright, with his gun in his hand. He was moving towards the far side of the roof, away from Roger and the others, walking crabwise, as if trying to watch them all at once.

One of the men on the other roof threw something – Roger couldn't see what it was. He shouted, but his voice was drowned in a clap of thunder. What were the fools playing at? If they hit Relf, he'd fall, and Roger wanted him alive. He shouted again, as something else was thrown; but the shout was futile, the missile hit Relf and he lost his balance.

The end came suddenly.

He screamed, missed his footing and plunged over.

The fools – to kill him! They weren't worth their rank, whatever it was; they were utter idiots.

Roger heard nothing more from Relf. The roof seemed empty, the night a void – until he saw the two men hurrying away. Then the truth flashed upon him; those two weren't detectives, and they had deliberately sent Relf to his death.

He turned away – and a man moved near him and spoke cheerfully.

"Got a story for me, Handsome?"

Roger started; his anger about the trick fell upon this man's head.

"How the hell did you get here?"

"Persistence, unexpected agility, and a nose for news," said the other easily. It was the tubby *Echo* reporter named Clayton. "I thought I was doing the right thing by coming up, but now I wish I was down below. Coming?"

Chapter Ten

Rose

Drenched men stood about the garage, looking dejected and grim when Roger entered. He had climbed through a roof-light in the next building and come down the stairs. He had glanced at Relf's broken body, which was now being placed in an ambulance. Near the door, moving away, were two detectives and the fellow who had uttered the uncanny gibberish while hurling missiles.

Most of the raiding force were now in the garage. A man came up to Roger with a fairly dry towel.

"Better use this, sir," he said.

"Thanks, I could do with a hot drink," said Roger.

"Brew of tea coming from a café across the road, sir."

"Good." Roger towelled vigorously, hands, face, and hair. His clothes clung to him, wet, uncomfortable. He spoke as he dried himself, using short, brisk sentences.

"We could have done worse," he said. "Another man has gone where he can't do any harm. I expect you know that a couple of his buddies slipped past us. Went up on the roof next door and sent him to Kingdom Come."

Men nodded and grunted, and some looked sheepish.

Roger said: "It couldn't be helped – we're a mixed bunch, bound to be some men others wouldn't recognise. Easy enough for outsiders with cool nerves to mix with us."

A burly man volunteered: "I think I saw them, sir, but they had their hats pulled down over their eyes. I thought what lucky beggars they were to have macks."

"The night helped 'em," Roger agreed. "We've got one man and the girl." He glanced at the office. "Where are they?"

"Across the road, in a café," said Peel, who had just come in. "Thought we'd get 'em out of here."

"Quite right. Has Rose talked?"

"Not a squeak," said the burly man. "And the other one is—"

Two men appeared at the door, carrying a tray on which were a dozen or so cups of steaming tea. One was a Yard officer, the other a little fellow in a dirty white apron, an Italian café proprietor judging from his sallow face, long chin, and dark, lank, greasy hair.

Roger drank his tea and put the cup on the wing of a cab.

"That was good. Now—"

"I was saying, sir," said the burly man, "the other beggar won't be much good tonight. He's deaf and dumb. Isn't it true, Guiseppe?"

The Italian spread out his hands.

"Yes, pliz, Tommy no spika, no listen." He went off into a long discourse; obviously he knew the garage and its staff and patrons well, and he was worth listening to.

Wignall was the owner, who usually left about eight o'clock. Relf was in charge during the night, and went off duty at seven o'clock in the morning. He was a skilled mechanic.

The man Tommy was a deaf-mute.

He had no home, was just a human derelict whom Relf had allowed to sleep on a heap of rags in the loft. That explained his wild fury when Relf had been in danger. The Italian also knew most of the taxi-drivers who put their cabs in this garage. They were all owner-drivers, Wignall wouldn't take any others. Among them was a man named Kirby, and when Roger showed the Italian a photograph of Kirby, Guiseppe nodded vigorously. Then he described the cab, and made it clear that the man who called himself 'Smith' had been in Kirby's cab that afternoon. He was a friend of Kirby's.

Guiseppe's café was immediately opposite, and obviously he missed little that went on in the garage. He didn't know the name of Kirby's friend, but had noticed that he usually came at night, when Relf was on duty. Rose was Kirby's girl.

"That's fine, Guiseppe," said Roger. "That's a great help – we won't forget it. And we won't worry you any more than we can help."

"Poliss bad for da bizzniss," Guiseppe declared, and gave a curiously attractive grin. "Pliz, da cabbies are not many badda boys. Kirby no lika dem, dey no lika Kirby; only Relf lika Kirby."

Roger nodded and turned to Peel.

"Where's the girl?"

"Rosa in my caff ay," said Guiseppe. "I giva da food, and giva poor Tommy da food. If I do not, he no eat."

"Lucky for Tommy that you're around," said Roger.

He detailed two men to search the office. The thunder rumbled away in the distance. Lights blazed from Guiseppe's café. Roger pushed open the door, making a bell clang harshly. A plump little woman appeared in another doorway, leading to a room at the back of the shop. Her dark hair was plaited, her cheeks were red and rosy.

"My Guiseppe good man!" she declared breathlessly.

"I'm sure of that," said Roger.

"Shutta da mouth, Marta," ordered Guiseppe. "Getta more tea, pliz, hurry. Tea for all da polissmans." He smacked his wife's arm lightly as he led Roger into the back room.

Two detectives were standing by the fireplace, the woman Rose was sitting in a winged arm-chair in a corner, glaring sullenly in front of her, and 'poor Tommy' crouched, terrified, in another corner. He was dressed in rags, his hair was long and unkempt, his fingers were like blackened talons. As Roger moved towards him, he sprang up and cowered back against the wall.

Roger turned to Peel.

"Get him to Cannon Row, and then get hold of someone who can talk to him."

Peel and another man took Tommy off. Guiseppe brought more tea on a tray, but the girl waved him away. Roger sipped his, and had half finished it before he said: "Not a very good day for you, Rose. When did you last see Kirby?"

"I haven't seen him all day!" she cried in a harsh, emotional voice. "It's no use asking me anything about Kirby. I won't talk!"

"That's asking for trouble," Roger said quietly. "Look here, Rose, you won't help anyone by being difficult. We aren't trying to pin anything on you—"

"You're trying to pin it on Kirby. But you won't get him – see? You won't get him. He's smarter than any dick in London." She jumped up from her chair. "I won't talk, you'll never get him!"

Guiseppe clucked. "Badda girl, Rosa!"

"Kirby was murdered this afternoon," Roger said bluntly. Rose drew back. The colour drained from her face, behind the make-up.

Guiseppe called in a strained voice: "Marta! Marta! Getta da brandy, quick!"

Rose said softly, sighingly: "That's a lie."

"It isn't a lie. He shot a policeman. Then he went off to join his friend, who was in a car nearby. The friend ran over him."

"It's a lie!" she screamed, and flew at Roger, took his wrists and gripped them tightly. "It isn't true," she gasped. "You're lying to me; you're just trying to make me talk!"

Roger said: "The body's in the morgue now."

She didn't move for what seemed a long time, but at last she sagged away from him, groped for a chair and dropped into it. She began to shiver, and Guiseppe came forward with some brandy in a glass; but Roger touched his shoulder and shook his head.

"Wait," he murmured, then raised his voice: "Rose, we're after the man who murdered Kirby. We were after Kirby, but we can't do him any harm now. Nor can you. The man who killed him sometimes took his cab out – he had it out this afternoon. I want to know all about him. Let's have the story, and then you can get some rest."

She didn't answer at first, but suddenly she began to talk – and what she said was dreadful and obscene. She called Kirby's murderer everything foul that she could think of, and the tirade went on for several minutes. When she finished, she leaned back and closed her eyes, as if exhausted.

Roger said: "You're about right, Rose, that's why we want him. What's his name? Where does he live?"

Her lips moved, as if talking were now an effort.

"I dunno where he lives," she said. "His name's Mike. Mike Scott. I'll tear his bloody eyes out. I'll make him—" She jumped up and began to scream, and this time Roger took her roughly by the shoulders, forced her to sit down again, and beckoned Guiseppe. He stood over her while she drank the brandy. She was in no state to be left on her own that night, so he instructed the detectives to take her to Bow Street Police-Station.

All the time he was thinking of the wanted man's name – not Smith, but Scott; and a Jeremiah Scott already figured in this affair.

Roger signed a bill which Guiseppe prepared for him, arranged for four men to stay at the garage to question any late-arrival taxi-drivers, and then went off in his own car to Chelsea. By the time he reached Bell Street he was taken with a fit of the shivers, and hoped he hadn't caught a chill. It was a fine night now, although much cooler.

Shivering, he took his keys out of his damp pocket and opened the door. He'd have to disturb the two women; he must put on dry clothes – and what wouldn't he give for a hot bath! He glanced at his watch when he switched on the hall-light. It was just after two. The thermostat would heat the bath water in half an hour or so. He crept into the kitchen and switched on the heater, and then filled a kettle. He banged the kettle against the taps, and scowled at his clumsiness; that would probably wake Janet. He heard no sound, however. There was a bath-towel in the airing cupboard in a corner of the kitchen, and he took off his clothes and began to towel himself vigorously – no hope of getting warm, until he was dry. Gradually he started to glow. The kettle was beginning to sing.

He turned to lower the gas – and as he did so a draught caught him, sharp and cold. The door was opening. He saw a man's head. He grabbed a cup from the table, ready to throw. Then the head came farther into the room – a crop of brown hair and his own silk dressing-gown!

"Noisy devil," said this apparition. "Can't a man sleep?"

Roger lowered the cup. "Mark, you ass!"

"That's right, be offensive when I've been keeping your makeshift bed warm," complained the other. He came in and closed the door. "Man in all his nakedness, eh? Get caught in the storm?"

"I went for a swim," said Roger.

Janet had told him on the telephone that Mark Lessing had wanted to know if he would be back before midnight; hopefully, he had shaken down on the camp-bed.

Lessing was tall and lean, good-looking in a way which made most people think that he was austere, even aloof. He collected old china and wrote books about it. China was his passion, but he had a secondary interest which at times superseded the first – he studied murder from every angle, including the psychological. Occasionally, he 'helped' Roger, and he could apply his theoretical knowledge expertly. From the beginning he had been interested in the Randall case.

"You must be pretty tired," he observed. "You go and tuck into bed – Jan's left your pyjamas out for you – and I'll bring you some tea. Me for an arm-chair for the rest of the night, and no argument."

"You can have the bed," said Roger dryly. "I'm going out again. That'll teach dilettantes like you the difference between dabbling and doing."

"Hot bath, hot whisky, with a lump of sugar in it, that's what you want," said Mark.

"Get me the whisky, will you?" asked Roger.

He went upstairs with the towel draped round his shoulders, and closed the bathroom door before turning on the hot tap. The room was soon filled with steam, and he soaked for ten minutes in the bath before Mark arrived with the hot whisky and sugar.

"Any sound from the bedroom?" Roger asked.

"No. Why?"

"Clothes—"

"Wear mine," said Mark promptly. "I can borrow one of your suits in the morning."

"I'll never be able to say you're always short of ideas again," said Roger.

He dressed in the dining-room.

"Nothing I can do in this, is there?" asked Mark.

"Just pop out in the morning and find Sybil Lennox," said Roger lightly. "No, I shouldn't want you to stick your neck out in this job. I don't like it a little bit."

Chapter Eleven

The Mute

Roger didn't go straight to the Yard, but turned into Cannon Row Police Station. Peel was in the charge-room with an elderly clergyman.

"Mr Cartwright's from the Deaf and Dumb Association, sir," Peel said.

"Very good of you to come, sir," said Roger. "Have you seen the man Tommy?"

Cartwright shook his head.

"You know why we want to question him, I suppose?"

"This gentleman says someone has been killed. I do hope this unfortunate man isn't suspected."

"No, not personally."

Roger went into a brief account of Tommy's known history and his association with the murdered man. Cartwright kept nodding, and when the story was finished he said: "I'll help, gladly. Perhaps I can also help the man."

"Let's hope so," said Roger. "The best thing is for us to write you out a list of questions we want answered, and you to try to get Tommy to tell you the truth."

"As a matter of fact, I've started on a list," said Peel.

"Good, let's have a look at it."

There wasn't much to add to the questionnaire, and Roger went along to get Tommy.

The deaf-mute was in the small rest-room. He still crouched in a corner, as if that were a natural position for him, and looked as unkempt and derelict as he had at the café.

Roger was fascinated when these two met. It wasn't just Cartwright's smile, but more the clergyman's general expression, the way he came forward and took Tommy's arm. As if by a miracle, Tommy was soothed. Then Cartwright's fingers began to move, slowly, as if he realised that Tommy's knowledge of the deaf-and-dumb language was likely to be scanty and imperfect. But Tommy held up his hands and made some kind of answer. The talon-like finger-nails were revolting as they clicked together.

Then Cartwright turned to Roger.

"Please leave us together, Mr West. He will talk more freely if we're alone."

"All right," said Roger, and pointed to a bell-push. "Ring when you've finished, please."

He went out to join Peel in the passage.

They went across to the Yard, and the first thing he saw was the report from the ballistics experts.

The bullets taken from Randall's body were identical in size and barrel-markings with those taken from Goodwin's chest. Randall had been shot by the same gun – Kirby's gun.

Just after five o'clock, word came from Cannon Row that the Rev Cartwright had done all he could. Roger went across and found him despondent. Apparently Relf had been the deaf-mute's only friend. Tommy had 'lived' at the garage for over a year. He claimed to know nothing of Relf s activities, but had realised that his benefactor was in danger and had tried desperately to help him.

"He may know more, Mr West, but I sincerely doubt it," said Cartwright. "And I'm worried about him, I really am. He's smothered with lice and filth, he needs decontaminating thoroughly. I have facilities at the hostel, and beg you to allow me to take him away."

"If you'll accept responsibility for him, take him," said Roger. "We can't help him – you might be able to."

Cartwright looked astounded.

"Are you serious?"

"Yes, of course."

Cartwright squeezed Roger's arm.

"I shall always remember this, Mr West. I didn't expect it at all. You're very kind – most humane."

Roger grinned. "Well, I can guarantee that we're human!"

Twenty minutes later the pair had gone. A police-car followed them as a matter of routine. When the car had turned out of the gates, Peel rubbed his eyes and said: "Are we really as hard as Cartwright seemed to think?"

"I'm beginning to wonder myself," said Roger. "Forget it. We must put a call out for Michael Scott, and I want to see Jeremiah Scott tomorrow. Might be a coincidence in names, but—" He broke off, for speculation was pointless.

The office work done, Roger drove to Wignall's garage, but the men there had drawn a blank; there were no papers to help the police. A taxi-driver had telephoned Wignall, who arrived shortly afterwards. He was a chunky man who had little to say, and swore that he knew nothing about Relf's private affairs.

Then Roger went to see Relf's body. The neck was broken, and death had been instantaneous.

The contents of his pockets had been put in a heap by his side; there was little of interest, except his home address. A detective had already gone there, and found a two-roomed flat over some mews; but nothing came of a search there.

It was well past seven o'clock when Roger reached home, after a telephone call to the hospital; Goodwin had passed a comfortable night.

Roger slept from half-past eight until one o'clock, had a hurried lunch at home, went to the Yard to find nothing helpful had come in, and drove straight to Tucktos.

The sprawling mass of buildings that was the main factory and printing works of Tucktos Limited spread over one of the north-western suburbs of London, forty minutes by road from Scotland Yard. Roger was admitted by a uniformed commissionaire at the iron gates, for the whole of the factory grounds were walled or railed off. Lorries, several of them loaded with great rolls of paper, were standing about a huge shed.

Once inside the building, Roger had a very different impression of it. The square entrance-hall was panelled with light oak; behind a desk three smartly dressed girls were sitting.

Upstairs there was a huge office with glass walls, in which some two hundred people were working. A passage ran practically the whole length of the office, and on the other side were small offices, most of them also with glass walls. Two, at the far end, had wooden partitions, however, and the first door was marked: *I Deverall, Sales Director.*

A middle-aged woman opened the door.

"Please, Miss Grey, this is *Inspector* West," breathed the boy who was guiding Roger.

"Oh yes, Inspector! Come in." Miss Grey led Roger across a small room to another door. She opened it and announced him.

Two men were in the room beyond – one behind a flat-topped desk which was littered with papers and samples of boxes, one sitting in an easy chair in front of it. The first man was in his shirt-sleeves. He was probably in the middle thirties, although thick horn-rimmed glasses made him look older.

"Afternoon, Inspector. Cigarette?" He pushed a box across the desk and knocked some papers off; the secretary picked them up and then went out. "Sit down," Deverall went on. "Still hot, isn't it?" He flicked a lighter and Roger leaned forward to take the light. "Well, what can we do for Scotland Yard? Not often we have the chance to help."

His rather hard voice, his brusque manner, a peculiar air of condescension, all struck the wrong note. But Roger thought less of him than of the other man, who slouched back in his chair, with a smile that was half a sneer on his thin, rather gaunt face.

So this was Jeremiah Scott, easily recognisable from his description.

Roger said formally: "Not often I've any cause to come here, Mr Deverall."

"I should damn well think not!" said Deverall. "What's afoot?"

"I'm CID *Criminal* investigation, and I want to get in touch with a member of your Sales Staff, a Mr Jeremiah Scott." Roger was still very formal.

"Just imagine that," drawled Scott.

His voice was mellow and pleasant, quite unexpected from this gangling man with the almost forbidding appearance.

Deverall rubbed his hands together.

"And he's right here, Inspector. There's luck for you!"

Roger started, as if he hadn't known, but Scott straightened up and took out a slim, gold cigarette-case.

"Don't pretend you didn't know I was here," he said. "What can I do for you?"

"I'd like to see you privately, Mr Scott," Roger said.

Deverall didn't argue.

"All right, if that's the way you want it. I'll call my secretary in, and you can use her office." He stood up and pressed a bell, and the woman came in immediately. "Your notebook, Miss Grey," said Deverall, and she bobbed out again. Deverall looked hard at Roger. "Inspector, I'm allowing this, but I hope it's nothing to do with Tucktos business. If it is, I've a right to know."

"If it is, you'll be told, sir."

Deverall flushed with annoyance.

In the small office, Scott lowered his long figure to the typist's chair, leaving an upright one for Roger, but Roger didn't take it.

"You knew Guy Randall, didn't you?" he asked.

"We'd met," Scott drawled.

"You met him on the day of his death, didn't you?"

"We met," said Scott again. "We didn't spend much time together, Inspector, and I only saw him *once* that day."

"Did he have anything to say to you?"

"No – he seldom did," Scott answered. He laughed – and the laugh, like his voice, was attractive. "Randall didn't get along with me. He didn't believe in mixing business with pleasure and two whiskies in an evening were his limit …"

"Weren't you rivals?"

"Rivals?" Scott's eyebrows shot up. "I wouldn't say that – if you mean I wanted his girlfriend, I just don't like that kind."

"How well do you know Sybil Lennox?"

"More than enough."

"Did Randall know that you and she were acquainted?"

"I couldn't say. Probably he did. But I knew her before she came up in the world. Like to know where, Inspector? Anmere RAF Station. Believe it or not, I was a bomber pilot and she was in the operations room. She thought too much of herself then, but when she started to get among wealthy friends, she thought she was God's special gift to men."

Roger might have been ages discovering that the girl and Scott were acquainted; but in spite of the man's frankness, he felt that Scott was amusing himself, almost mocking him. That might be just the nature of the man.

"You and Randall were in competition with each other – you were rivals in a business sense, weren't you?" Roger asked.

"He thought so," said Scott.

"Didn't you?"

Scott leaned forward. "I've forgotten more about selling than that cluck would ever have known," he asserted. "In any case, the Crown people aren't *printers*. They've got a little rabbit hutch up near Birmingham, and they're trying to run before they can walk. You couldn't call it competition."

"But you didn't like it."

"I didn't give a damn," said Scott lazily.

"Not when he took Perriman's order from you?"

Scott let the smoke curl from his mouth and make a veil in front of his eyes.

"Randall didn't take that from me," he said slowly. "Sam Perriman did. He's a total abstainer, and I'm not." He grinned. "I was invited to the Perriman Staff Dance, and there was some drink around. I took more than was good for me, and Mr Samuel didn't like it. I told him where to get off. As a result, he wanted to place an order quickly, and gave it to the first person who came along."

"I see," Roger said. "You had no grudge against Randall?"

"No, and if I had, I wouldn't have shot him," said Scott. "But he was playing with fire when he mixed with Sybil Lennox and her friends. Why don't you ask Sybil to introduce you to those friends, West?"

Scott had deliberately led the conversation back to the girl.

"Don't you read the newspapers?" Roger asked abruptly.

"I haven't seen one today, if that's what you mean," said Scott. "Why?"

"We're looking for Sybil Lennox. She's disappeared."

"Has she, by jingo! I—"

The telephone bell rang jarringly, and Scott broke off. The door opened and Miss Grey said: "It's a call for you, Mr Scott."

"Oh, thanks. Sorry we've been interrupted," said Scott insincerely, and stretched for the receiver. "Yes, what is it? Speak up, I can't hear you … Oh, *Mike*. Yes, what … Oh, are you?"

His voice altered. He shot Roger a single, vivid glance and looked hastily away again; he hadn't meant to show his feelings – his alarm. And that 'Mike' could well refer to Michael Scott.

Roger took out a cigarette and stifled a yawn. Scott relaxed a little. He kept saying: "Yes … yes, old boy." And then finally: "Sure, I'll come along one day, sure. 'Bye, old chap."

He rang off.

"Customer wants to see me," he declared, and that was a palpable lie.

Chapter Twelve

Life in the Balance

Mike Scott, his face still patched, his hand bandaged, and his right eye turning a bluish purple, put down the receiver. Two other men were with him, biggish fellows with hard, unshaven faces. They were sitting on either side of a small dining-table on which cards lay.

"He coming?" asked one of the men.

Mike said: "Yeah, he's coming if I ring again. He sounded cagey."

"Meaning what?"

"How the hell do I know what it means?" demanded Mike.

"Mike, we've got to get some dough," said one of the men. "We can't touch yours, it ain't safe, and we can't get none through Relf any more. Your brother—"

"My brother never has enough dough," said Mike. "He'll find some, though. We're safe enough here, aren't we? I can lie low until my face is mended. What's the matter with you two going and earning some money, anyway?"

One man said: "We're not going out, Mike, don't make any mistake about that. We did the job, didn't we? We got rid of Relf."

"And I got rid of Kirby, that makes us even." Mike Scott gave a hard, little laugh, but wasn't amused. "Someone's got to go out."

"We did our job—" the man began.

"Shut up talking about your job!" cried Mike. "Kirby fixed Randall and got the case, Kirby was the man who made contact with the Boss, and now Kirby's gone we don't know who the Boss is or how to get in touch with the shyster. The Boss told me to see that Kirby wasn't nabbed; he told you to see that Relf wasn't nabbed, and we fixed it. But where's that got us? Maybe we'll never hear from the Boss again."

A bell rang.

One of the men jumped up. "What's that?"

"How the hell do I know?" growled Mike. "Topsy will see."

They were in the middle one of three rooms. It had only a small window overlooking a tiny back garden and a wooden fence. The glass was frosted. An indoor passage ran alongside the room, and a woman padded along it towards the front door. They could imagine her blowsy, frowsy figure.

They heard the door open and a man's voice. The front door closed, and the man spoke again, so the woman had admitted him. The door of the room opened and the woman said: "Someone to see yer."

A man came in.

He was short and wore a beard. Just an ordinary, neat, dark beard with a few streaks of grey. He had a big moustache, too, and his eyebrows were bushy and his hair plentiful. He wore a light raincoat, and beneath it a black coat and waistcoat and striped trousers.

None of the men in the room knew him; none had seen him before. He smiled, just a little movement of his lips, and put a small attaché-case on the sideboard. He glanced at the dirty crockery and at the table.

It was Mike who broke the silence in a cracked voice.

"Who are you, behind that beard and grease-paint?"

"Shall we say a friend?" asked the bearded man. "I thought I would come myself, because you must all be feeling very worried. We've had a bad spell."

The big man muttered: "Are you the Boss?"

"Just call me a friend," said the bearded man in his pleasant voice. "I know what you've done, and I must say you've handled it very well indeed. You know, both Relf and Kirby were becoming difficult. They weren't reliable, not like you. Kirby bungled the job at our lady friend's room, didn't he? All I asked was for him to plant the brief-case there quietly, and he had to let the police know he'd broken in. His nerves weren't very good, were they, Mike?"

Mike Scott said: "I suppose not."

"And then there was Relf, kicking up that scene in the Strand," said the bearded man. "It wouldn't have been so bad if he'd stopped at talking, but to kick that policeman simply shouted that it was a trick. However, you three did very well. Mixing with those policemen last night took some nerve. Mike will have to stay in hiding for a little while – till his face heals up."

He took out a wad of notes.

"Here's a hundred," he said. "Split it even. That's just to tide you over, of course, there's plenty more where it came from. We're doing *very* well."

Mike took the notes; the two big men eyed them hungrily.

"Yeah, but just what *are* we doing?" demanded Mike.

The bearded man smiled.

"My dear Mike, the less you know the better. You are told exactly what to do, and you get well paid for it. That's an excellent arrangement. Kirby knew a little more, and so did Relf – that's why they became rather difficult. Divide the money, Mike, or the others will think you're trying to take more than your share!"

Mike slowly counted out the money – two lots of thirty-three pounds. He left one on the table and said: "Topsy can have that."

The rest he pocketed.

The other men took their cut.

"I'm going to send for you, Mike, after dark," said the bearded man. "The taxi's all right, that won't be found yet – and when it is, it'll be a different colour." He smiled. "If it weren't for one person, I'd be thoroughly happy. I don't know what to say about her, it depends on whether you boys think she'll keep her mouth shut."

The big man snapped: "Mean Topsy?"

"Oh no, Topsy is all right," the other said smoothly. "I'm thinking about the girl upstairs. I don't like killing, it's always bad when we have to resort to it, but one more wouldn't make any difference. And you'd feel safer. She doesn't know *me,* so I've nothing to fear from her. You have. You couldn't tell the police anything about me even if you wanted to, so it's for you to decide. The only thing I ask is – if you decide she'll be better out of the way – be quick about it."

They nodded, and the bearded man glanced at the ceiling.

Sybil Lennox was in the room above.

"You might make it look like suicide," he went on thoughtfully. "It should be possible to leave something there to make it appear that she killed Randall too."

"The dicks have got Kirby's gun," said Mike.

"They know he shot at the policeman, they don't know that the gun was his. They'd have a job!" He gave a little laugh. "It belonged to Sybil, she was once persuaded that she needed one for her own protection. If a few bullets to fit the gun were left in her room it would be helpful. The police always see the obvious, even if they miss everything else. After all, they found some of the contents of Randall's brief-case in her room. And she ran away. If she's dead, she can't tell the police why she ran, can she? In case you want the bullets, here they are." He put a small brown-paper packet on the table. "Mike, I shall send for you just after dark. You others can leave whenever you like – Topsy had better leave early too."

The big man asked: "Where can we find you?"

"Oh no, that won't do – I'll find *you*," said the bearded man. "But instead of calling at Wignall's garage for messages, call at Joe's saloon in the Mile End Road."

He went out of the room, short, straight as a ramrod, stepping briskly.

When the front door closed on him, three pairs of eyes turned towards the ceiling.

Mike said: "We'll have to fix her."

"Not so easy," said the big man. "The dicks can smell a fake suicide miles off."

"There's a gas-fire in her room," said the third man.

"Listen to me," said the big man. "You and me can leave this place when we want to – he wouldn't have pulled a fast one over that. We can scram."

"That's right."

"Mike can't," the man said meaningly.

Mike Scott flicked his lighter, lit a cigarette. His left hand strayed to his face, and he began to pick at a piece of adhesive plaster.

"So you reckon I can hold the baby." He gave an ugly little laugh. "We could just slit her throat."

"You aren't going to get away with that," said the big man roughly. "We've been seen coming in here, and maybe we'll be seen going out. It's got to be suicide."

"Could try," yawned Mike. "It would mean putting her to sleep and then turning on the gas. How are we going to get her to sleep?" He gave the ugly little laugh again. "Beaver didn't think of that one, did he?"

The big man said softly: "Didn't he?" He put his hand to his waistcoat pocket and drew out a small glass tube – like a cheap tube of aspirins. He uncorked it and shook two or three tiny white tablets on to his great, sweating palm. "That's morphia. He knew I had some."

Sybil Lennox stirred restlessly on the big double bed.

She was lying at full length, her arms folded over her head, her eyes narrowed as she looked at the small window opposite the bed. Her shoes lay on the floor; over her legs, from the knees downwards, was a bright pink eiderdown. The room was hideously furnished and had a flowered wallpaper. She knew that the house was in Hurlingham, in a side-street not far from the tennis club, but knew little else about it.

She had been brought here the previous night by Mike, whom she knew well and who had given her her orders for some time. Except when Mike had looked in for a few minutes late the previous night, she had seen only the two men and the slatternly old woman called Topsy. Topsy had brought her supper, breakfast, and lunch. Sybil knew that she would soon be told what to do next, knew that she would have to obey – it was useless to act on her own initiative.

She heard the stairs creak.

It was nearly five o'clock – she had been here just on twenty-four hours.

The creaking grew louder and she heard the shuffling footsteps of the woman. Topsy came in, carrying a tray and breathing heavily. She dumped the tray on the chair, and some tea spilled out of the spout of the tea-pot. There was a plate of bread and butter, the bread thick and stale, the butter scraped; that was all, except the milk and sugar. Topsy shuffled out.

Sybil looked at the bread and butter distastefully, then more cheerfully at the tea-pot. She stretched out for the milk-jug, then saw that there was some milk in the cup. She didn't give a second thought to that, but poured out tea and put in two spoonfuls of sugar. She sipped; the tea was very strong, so she added more sugar. She nibbled at a piece of bread and butter, finished the tea and poured out another cup.

It wasn't long afterwards that she began to feel drowsy.

In half an hour she was asleep.

She was lying there, breathing evenly, when Mike came in. He stood looking at her, with a twisted smile. He shook her arm, then her shoulder, but she didn't stir. He slapped her across the face sharply. The blow left a red mark which gradually faded, but it didn't rouse her. He gave that soft, ugly laugh, and put on a pair of cotton gloves. He crossed to the dressing-table on which lay her handbag, and took from his pocket the little packet containing the bullets – three in all. He slipped them into the bag.

Then he went to the gas-fire, where there was a gas-ring with a long flex. He disconnected the ring so that the tubing flex was free, and brought an old arm-chair to the fireplace. As he did that, footsteps sounded in the hall and the front door closed.

He paused, staring at the door. He was now alone in the house with Sybil.

He shrugged his shoulders and turned to the girl on the bed. He carried her to the fireplace and put her on the floor near the gas-ring; then bent down, took her hand in his, and made her turn on the tap. Gas hissed out. He held her thumb and forefinger tightly over the tap and turned it off; her fingerprints would be clear enough on it now. Then he dragged her near the chair, her head resting against it, and pushed her so that the tubing stretched to her mouth without being too taut. But it wouldn't stay there. He looked round and saw a tall, oak towel-rail in a corner near the old-fashioned, marble-topped wash-stand.

He brought it near the chair and rested the tubing on it. Now it pointed straight at her face. He lifted her into the chair, and then drew the tubing closer, so that it was within an inch of her mouth, which was slightly open. He took her hand again, and closed her fingers round the tubing – her prints would be on there too.

He stood back, to admire his handiwork.

Sybil's hair, a golden cascade, covered part of the tube. The cheek he had slapped was a glowing pink, but the other was pale. She looked as nearly beautiful as ever she would.

Mike went to the gas-tap, bent down, touched the edge of the tap and pushed it gently, so as not to smear or blur her prints. He went to the window and drew the curtains, then went out and closed the door.

Chapter Thirteen

Jeremiah Scott Pays a Call

Half an hour after West had left the Tucktos office, Jeremiah Scott left Deverall and went out to the car-park. His car was a powerful, grey Chrysler, modern, glittering, and stream-lined. He looked about him carefully when he turned into the main road, but saw no sign of West. It was twenty-five past five when eventually he found himself in Hurlingham. He pulled up in a side-road, took out a book-map of London streets and found Kent Street, the name of the road his brother had mentioned over the telephone. He drove swiftly to Kent Street and pulled up a few doors away from number 41, for which he was looking. He sat in the car for a few minutes, looking round constantly, until he was certain that no one was watching him, then he got out and went to number 41.

He banged the heavy brass knocker.

No one answered, and he knocked again and rang the bell. There was still no answer.

He tried once more, but only silence greeted him. He turned away from the porch and went into the small front garden – and then he stood quite still, shocked into immobility.

West and two other men were approaching from one direction and two big fellows, with 'plain-clothes officers' written all over them, were coming from the other. A uniformed constable stood by the Chrysler.

After the first shock, Jeremiah Scott forced a grin.

Roger turned in at the gate.

"Paying a call?" he asked casually.

"Since when have I to ask permission to call on friends?" retorted Scott.

"You haven't," Roger assured him. He smiled at Scott's glaring face. "Don't get worked up," he said. "While I was with you, your brother Michael telephoned you. We want to interview him – and it seemed that you might be planning to see him. Yes?"

Scott made no answer.

"Let's see if we can make them hear," said Roger.

He went to the door and gave a heavy knock, which echoed along the street; but there was no response, and Scott's grin broadened.

"I thought I might find a customer in," said Scott airily. "But it's not our lucky day, is it, West?"

"There's a lot of the day left yet," said Roger. He turned to Peel, who was just behind him. "Our other chaps will be at the back by now, won't they?"

"Ages ago," said Peel.

"All right, let's see what we can do," said Roger.

"Got permission to break in?" asked Scott.

"Yes," said Roger shortly.

He examined the lock of the door while his men examined the windows, all with a deliberation which seemed to afford Scott a cynical amusement. Meanwhile Peel had found that he could open the window of the front room by slipping a knife between the frame and the catch. He threw the window up.

As he did so there was a bellow at the back of the house; a pause, and then a shrill blast of a police-whistle. "Got someone!" cried Peel.

"Watch Scott!" Roger snapped to one of his men, and followed as Peel climbed through the window. There was no noise in the house, but the whistle shrilled out again and they could hear voices. Roger reached the passage first, then rushed along the side of the staircase. The kitchen door was shut. He turned the handle but the door was locked; and he put his shoulder to the panels and heaved. It made no impression. Peel came up, and they tried between them, but couldn't shift the door. There were sounds of scuffling inside – but the noise stopped abruptly and the door was unlocked by a detective, whose hair was dishevelled and who had a scratch on his right cheek, but who said triumphantly: "Got him, sir!"

"Who?"

"Michael Scott – well, he's all done up with sticking-plaster and his right hand's bandaged, I'm pretty sure it's him."

"That's fine," said Roger. "Now we can bring the brothers face to face."

He looked past the Yard man to the scullery door, through which Mike was being hustled by two more detectives. Mike's nose was bleeding at the tip and he was breathing hard; it was as if he knew that this was the first step on the road to the gallows. Jeremiah Scott was in the hall.

He caught his breath when he recognised his brother. But obviously neither he nor Roger were prepared for the sudden outburst of vituperation which poured from Mike's lips.

"You ruddy witless fool, you brought them here!" He spat the words out. "I'd like to cut your throat, you've shopped me, you …"

He went on and on, and Jeremiah Scott, for once not smiling, stood quite still and stared at him.

At last Roger said sharply: "That's enough." He looked at Peel. "Handcuff him, and then let's look through the house. I want you to stay," he added to Jeremiah, who had taken out his gold cigarette-case, and proffered it to his brother. Mike took a cigarette, the last thing he did before the handcuffs were slipped over his wrists. He gave a grin that was almost shamefaced.

"Don't say a word," advised Jeremiah. "Don't give anything away, Mike. I'll get a good lawyer."

Mike nodded, his rage forgotten.

The gas was hissing softly.

They found no one in the ground-floor rooms, but some playing-cards were on the table in the middle room, and a pile of dirty crockery was on a chair – evidence that several people had been there.

Roger and Peel went upstairs. As soon as they reached the landing, Roger put a hand on Peel's arm, a gesture of urgency.

"Smell that? It's gas. Come on!"

They found Sybil Lennox just as Mike had left her, in a gas-filled room.

Twenty minutes later the doctor arrived. Sybil had been taken into another bedroom, and was under a heap of bedclothes. The doctor grunted and bent a long stare at Roger.

"Kept her warm – good. Haven't tried artificial respiration, I hope."

"No, there wasn't much trace of breathing, it would only do harm. An ambulance is on the way."

"Good, good." The doctor began to open his case.

The ambulance arrived and Roger went downstairs, to where the brothers Scott were waiting in the front room. Neither of them had made any statement. Michael was tight-lipped and obviously frightened; Jeremiah gave Roger the impression of being more worried about his brother than himself. He was abrupt with both of them, and sent them to Cannon Row, after charging Mike Scott with driving a taxi-cab without a proper licence – which charge made Jeremiah pull down his long, lower lip in a cynical smile. He charged Jeremiah with 'withholding material evidence in connection with an offence.'

Peel came into the room while Roger was alone.

"Any word from upstairs?" asked Roger.

"No, they're still busy."

"Having quite a time, aren't we?" asked Roger. "What's in the room where we found Sybil Lennox?"

"Not much," said Peel cautiously. "She handled the tubing and the gas-tap all right, but I can't find any other prints."

"Let's have a look," said Roger.

The tubing and the tap, as well as other things in the room, were smeared with grey powder. Roger studied the position of everything for a long time.

"Is she left-handed?" he asked.

"No report of that," said Peel.

"She isn't – she did everything right-handed when I saw her," said Roger, "and yet her thumb-print is where her forefinger print should be." He held the tubing while standing over the chair, and the grip was pretty well the same as the prints.

Peel's eyes glistened.

"She didn't do it herself, then?"

"No, I don't think so," said Roger. "She could hardly have been standing up and holding the tube. Look for the tiniest fraction of print from Mike's fingers, will you?"

"He probably wore gloves," said Peel, "but I'll have another go. I—but I'll tell you what, sir. I noticed several long, fair hairs on his waistcoat, fairly low down. If he lifted her—"

"They'll find them at Cannon Row," said Roger. "All right, get cracking."

He searched the room for papers, but found nothing of interest. Her handbag had the usual oddments, and – the bullets. He put them carefully away.

By the time he had finished, the men who had been searching downstairs had finished their job, and Roger found a little heap of papers and documents on a table in the front room. The house had been let furnished on a six months lease to 'Michael Scott,' whose address was given as Lanton Hotel, Bayswater. There were several letters to Michael, two from women, one from a bookmaker. That was all, except three pieces of folded paper which, when opened, proved to be programmes of matches played at Craven Cottage, the Fulham Football Club's ground. They were fortnightly – whoever had brought them had attended three successive home matches. The half-time scores were filled in, and two or three of the players names were scored with pencil markings.

"Not much there," said Peel. "Any idea what's behind it?"

"Damn-all," said Roger. "Except – we don't get murder laid on as thick as this because a man takes a dislike to another's face. I've been thinking of any big rackets, but I can't think of any this might touch, except – food. Perriman's are one of the biggest food firms in the country."

Just then a man came quickly down the stairs and Roger went to the door. It was a white-smocked ambulance man.

"She'll be all right, with luck," he said. "Thought you'd like to know."

Near neighbours were shocked by police questions and told varying stories, but some things emerged. A dowdy, old woman came in daily to the house, but no one knew her. A young, well-dressed girl had arrived in a taxi the previous evening – but no one could describe the taxi, although one man said he thought the driver had gone in with the girl and another man had driven the cab away.

No one mentioned the other two men, but several neighbours said they had seen a man loitering near the house the previous day. He was described as plumpish and dark-haired, and wore a black-and-white check coat and grey flannels. That struck a chord in Roger's mind but meant nothing to Peel.

Chapter Fourteen

Missing Man?

At a quarter-past seven, Roger reached Scotland Yard feeling that he couldn't complain about results.

Sybil Lennox would be well enough to talk next morning.

Roger walked along the cold corridors, meeting no one, and opened the door of his office. He smelt cigar smoke; the Assistant Commissioner smoked only cheroots or small cigars.

Chatworth looked up from Eddie Day's desk. He was in a dinner-jacket and smoking a cheroot.

"Oh, hallo, sir," said Roger brightly.

"Remember me?" Chatworth asked sourly. "Why haven't you been to see me today?"

"It's been a bit of a rush," said Roger defensively. "You've heard what happened at the garage—"

"Yes, all right," said Chatworth, who had obviously intended to be difficult, but now changed his mind. "Kirby – killed, murdered, *you* say, although every eye-witness seems to think it was an accident. You saw Relf murdered by being knocked off the roof, but he could have slipped. Michael Scott, missing for a while, but no real evidence that he was the driver of the taxi-cab. The girl, vanished. Not a very pleasing picture, is it?"

"We haven't got much for the Old Bailey yet, sir," said Roger, sitting on the next desk. "But there's a move forward. We can put

Scott up in the morning on a trivial charge and get a remand. We found the girl just in time to save her life."

Chatworth took the cheroot from his lips. "So you haven't been wasting all your time. How'd it happen?"

Roger gave a good outline of the story in ten minutes. Chatworth nodded with satisfaction and stood up. "Well, I'll leave it to you – but keep me informed."

"I will, sir."

Chatworth went off.

Roger crossed the yard to Cannon Row, where he found a solicitor named Greenwall with the Scott brothers. Greenwall was a first-class man with an irreproachable reputation. As Roger expected, he took the line that while the police had reason to hold Michael Scott, his brother was a different matter.

"I might agree, if he'd say why he went to see his brother," said Roger.

"Oh, he'll do that," said Greenwall, glancing at Jeremiah, who gave his half-sneering grin, and said that he had heard from Mike that he needed some money and was in trouble, and had gone straight to the house, because he wanted to help. He couldn't reasonably be detained any longer.

Roger said so.

"Then I'll have my worldly possessions back," said Jeremiah. "Your men took everything out of my pockets."

"That's normal enough," said Roger. "I'll get them."

The contents of Jeremiah's pockets were on a table in the Station superintendent's room. Roger glanced through them, and one thing in particular caught his attention. Jeremiah's gold cigarette-case was only one of many valuable items – everything there, in fact, might have been found in the pockets of a really wealthy man. Then he caught sight of a small folder, like a tiny book with a stiff cover. It was upside down when he first saw it, but he turned it round and read:

Membership Ticket. Fulham Football & Athletic Club, Ltd.

The sergeant put everything in a large envelope and Roger took them along with him to the charge-room. Jeremiah left soon afterwards. Mike, who had refused to make a statement, was lodged in the cells at the police-station, and Roger had a word with Greenwall, who asked lightly: "Having him up in the morning?"

"Yes, and I'll tell you in advance that I'm going to apply for a remand on the grounds that more serious charges are pending," said Roger. "That'll have to do you. I think you'll find that Michael Scott is deep in an ugly business."

Greenwall shrugged his shoulders and went off.

Peel was already busy at a microscope, looking at some fine golden-coloured hairs. Several had been taken from the back of the chair in which Sybil had been found, others from Mike's clothes; they were identical.

"We'll get him for attempted murder, anyhow," said Roger. "And I think I've placed the plump man who was seen at Kent Street. You saw him last night, didn't you? Soaked through, but in a black-and-white check coat."

"Clayton! The *Echo* reporter," said Peel.

"That's him," said Roger. "He got there ahead of us. Smart chap, Clayton. Oh, well. You get off."

Left alone, he found a fact constantly breaking into his thoughts. Three programmes of Fulham football matches at Kent Street, and a membership ticket for the same club in Jeremiah's pocket.

He reached Bell Street just after nine-fifteen, and Janet was at the door.

"Aren't I nice and early?" said Roger.

"You could have been later! Darling, some good news, they think Goodwin will be all right!"

"Thank God for that! Mrs Goodwin knows?"

"Yes, we've just come back from the hospital. She's upstairs – thank heavens, she's broken down now, and I thought she'd better get to bed early. You won't mind the camp-bed again, will you?"

Roger chuckled. "Again! I'd like to try it for a night."

Mark Lessing grinned at him from the doorway. From the kitchen came the smell of frying onions, and Roger heard someone moving about; their daily help had obviously 'stayed on.'

"Hungry?" asked Janet.

"Starving. You didn't wait dinner for me, did you?"

"No, yours is being cooked," said Janet. "It's a grill – hurry up and wash."

Roger ate in the dining-room. Janet sat at the table with him, drinking a cup of coffee. Mark Lessing lounged in an easy chair with his coffee-cup balanced precariously on the arm. Janet talked about the boys and Goodwin's daughter, Marjorie – they were getting on famously. Afterwards she went into the kitchen to help the woman with the washing-up, and Mark grinned lazily from his chair.

"Now let's have some inside dope, Roger. Found the girl?"

"Yes," said Roger. "That reminds me. I haven't seen much of the newspapers today. Let's go into the other room and see what they have to say."

The papers were full of the deaths of Kirby and Relf and the disappearance of Sybil Lennox. The *Echo* hinted darkly at organised crime. The report had been written by the Tommy Clayton who was so often on the spot.

Roger handed the paper to Mark.

"See anything much in that?" he asked.

"Oh, sheer guesswork."

"Clayton's a good guesser," Roger agreed. "Might be something in this."

"It's coming to something if the Yard wants a lead from the Press," remarked Mark.

"We get plenty," Roger said. He reached forward for the London telephone directory, ran his fingers down the columns until he came to the Claytons. Soon he dialled a number, and a woman answered him.

"Is Mr Clayton in, please?" asked Roger.

"Who is speaking?" The woman's voice was sharp.

"Inspector West of New Scotland Yard."

"And *you* want to know …" The woman caught her breath and then added tensely: "No, he hasn't been home since yesterday morning. I'm his wife. I'm afraid that something's happened to him."

"I expect he's been sent on a special job," said Roger soothingly. "I saw him last night."

"I telephoned the office," said the woman. "They say that he often stays away without telling them where he is, they don't think anything of it. But he *always* rings me up or sends me a wire. I really am worried."

"I can tell that you are," said Roger quietly. "Leave it with me, Mrs Clayton, I'll find out where he is."

He replaced the receiver and looked thoughtfully at Mark, then told him of Mrs Clayton's worry. Next, he telephoned the *Echo*. Yes, it was true that Clayton hadn't reported since sending in his report on the Randall case and the Relf business.

"And you can't help me to trace him?" said Roger.

"No, but Tommy's all right. He can look after himself."

Roger put down the receiver. He fiddled with the newspaper, thinking a great deal about the reporter who had first appeared in this case when he had tried to intercept Roger at the Yard. His arrival at Wignall's garage had seemed just quick work on the part of the newspaper, but if he had been in Kent Street that afternoon, if he was now missing …

The telephone bell rang, and he took off the receiver.

"Roger West speaking."

"Oh, West – *Echo* here again." It was the news-editor. "You've started me worrying about Clayton now. His wife was on the telephone earlier in the evening. Are you seriously worried?"

Roger said: "Yes."

"Well, I don't know what to make of it. Still, you'd better know that he believes that Perriman's, the food people, are concerned. He struck something when he was writing up some food monopoly and price-ring stuff. Didn't say much – he never does unless he can prove his case – but he thinks they might be a pretty bad lot."

"Perriman's?" murmured Roger. "Thanks, we'll check right away."

Chapter Fifteen

Truth From Sybil?

The curiously high cherry-red colour had faded from Sybil Lennox's face, leaving her very pale. She lay propped up on pillows, wearing a flannelette nightdress of hospital issue. Roger was by her side; a stenographer sat on the other side of the bed, and a woman police-sergeant stood in a corner. Roger said quietly: "I want you to tell me exactly what happened yesterday, Miss Lennox. Never mind about the day before. Why did you attempt to commit suicide?"

She started up. "But I didn't!"

"Oh, come," said Roger. "You—"

"It's not true! I don't remember what happened after I went to sleep and woke up here. I just don't remember. I didn't try to kill myself, why should I?"

"Do you know what happened to you?" asked Roger.

"A—a nurse told me I'd been gassed, but I had no idea. That dreadful woman brought me some tea yesterday afternoon. I felt drowsy, and – I didn't tell you!"

"So someone tried to murder you," said Roger quietly.

"Was it Mike Scott?" she demanded.

"He was at the house when we found you," said Roger.

"I suppose—I oughtn't to be surprised," said Sybil. "He took me there. He telephoned me after I—I'd had lunch with you at Sibley's. He persuaded me to go with him, and when we reached the house, he—made me stay."

"Made?" echoed Roger.

"Yes."

"Was he alone?"

"I didn't see anyone else except the old woman and two men – I only just caught a glimpse of the men. There was a visitor yesterday afternoon; I heard him come and heard him talking. They were in the room below mine. But I saw Mike, mostly."

"And you obeyed him," said Roger.

Sybil said: "I had to."

"Why?"

"He said—he could prove—I'd killed Guy," she declared very softly. "It wasn't true. Guy's death was—a terrible blow to me, but whoever killed him used—my gun."

She had first met Mike Scott at an RAF dance at Anmere. The dance hadn't been confined to the station staff, and Jeremiah Scott's brother had come. At the time, Sybil had rather liked Jeremiah, and certainly liked his brother. She'd spent a few short leaves with them in London – with another girl from the station.

Then she and Jeremiah had quarrelled.

Sybil's mother had died after nearly a year's illness, leaving Sybil on her own, with no close relatives, none whom she liked or with whom she could get on. But she had soon found the job with Boyd & Fairweather, and gone to Mrs Clarke's. Sometimes Mike Scott called to see her. He was married, and wanted her to live with him. When she'd refused, he'd turned sour.

Then she had answered an advertisement in a trade paper – a small firm wanted some drawings done by a freelance artist-draughtsman, and she had secured the job, adding to her already reasonable salary at Boyd & Fairweather's. She did more and more of this spare-time work, and the pay was extremely good. Messengers brought her the designs she was to copy and paid her in cash. She loved clothes, she wanted to accumulate some capital, and she worked extremely hard.

The drawings were varied. Sometimes of buildings, factories and warehouses, sometimes of small technical contraptions – engines, patent locks, a great variety of things. She did three identical drawings. For years she continued happily and cheerfully, meeting few friends because she spent so much time at her drawing-board – and then, suddenly, Mike had come to see her again and told her what she had really been doing.

Cracksmen studied the drawings, made models, learned how to force them; she was helping a band of criminals.

And she had been paid with stolen money.

She hadn't declared it as part of her income, either; but often it had been in five-pound notes, some of which could be traced. The amounts paid for each job had been far in excess of the usual fees, although she hadn't known it. In a short interval, Mike had shown that she was hopelessly involved. He had then wanted her to mix with prospective 'victims' of planned crimes, to prise information out of managers and others, or keep them occupied while the thieves were busy.

She had refused.

Then alarming things had happened. Her room had been entered and searched, she had been terrified in case the police had visited it. She was jostled from crowded pavements in the traffic-filled roads. It had seemed as if there was a campaign to break her nerve, and she was sure that Mike Scott was behind it. Once she had been cornered when walking along a dark, deserted street, and only saved from attack by a car which chanced to pass and frightened off her assailant. After that, she had bought a gun and some ammunition.

A friend had obtained it for her – one of her fellow boarders, who had left soon afterwards. She had realised too late that he was also one of Scott's friends, who had watched her and wormed his way into her confidence. She continued to do drawings for Scott, and among them had been copies of designs of Perriman's cartons and packages. She didn't know why. There had been designs for other commodities, Perriman's hadn't been the only firm. She was still paid for this work, and hadn't the courage to refuse to do it.

On Mike's orders, she went to Brighton for a weekend. There, she'd met Randall, at the hotel. She knew Mike had arranged that, but Mike hadn't reckoned on the result. They'd danced all the first evening, spent the Saturday and Sunday together, and fallen in love.

Realising this, Mike hadn't tried to make her 'work' anything on Randall.

She'd continued to see Randall in London – and then had discovered that she was followed wherever she went. One day her gun had been stolen from her handbag.

Two days later Randall had been killed.

And Mike had come to see her again, with the same demands. She was to be a decoy. He'd told her that her gun had been used in the murder, that if the police discovered who had owned it she was booked for the gallows. That was why she hadn't told the police the truth and had refused to admit that she was being followed.

Mike had telephoned to say that he must see her. She was to wait in the hall of the office block until a taxi drew up outside. Mike had taken her to the house in Hurlingham; she'd been locked in the upstairs room during the night, and told to stay there next day. She didn't know why, but had been terrified of disobeying.

When he had knocked the story into shape, Roger went to see Chatworth.

"Do you believe her?" Chatworth asked.

"Mostly, yes sir. Anyhow, we know that Scott's been the agent for a pretty big gang, don't we? And Kirby and Relf were in it. What I haven't fathomed yet is why Mike Scott suddenly decided to kill her."

"Sure it was him?" barked Chatworth.

Roger said: "We've got him on that all right. Her hairs were on his clothes, where he'd carried her. There was a smear or two of her powder on his coat too. But the most important thing was found on the gas-tap, sir – a section of his right forefinger print. The same tiny print section is on one of the bullets we found in the girl's bag too."

Chatworth nodded and grunted.

"It looks as if Sybil Lennox was weakening and would soon have taken Mike Scott's orders," said Roger. "Just at a time when he'd got her where he wanted her, he decided to get rid of her. He may have been afraid that she could say too much – or he may have acted on instructions. He's certainly not the leader of this crowd."

Chatworth grunted.

"The fact that she had to copy some Perriman cartons might mean a lot and might mean nothing at all," Roger went on. "The one real pointer is from her story of having to draw plans and diagrams. In several big food warehouse robberies, we've noticed that the thieves had a thorough knowledge of the layout – all doors and passages, for instance. I think we'll find that these robberies were carried out by the same mob. It wouldn't surprise me if this isn't what Tommy Clayton of the *Echo* was following up."

"Any news of him?"

"None at all," said Roger gloomily. "He was certainly in Kent Street."

"Fellow's probably trying to pull a fast one," said Chatworth. "What do you propose to do with the girl?"

"I think she ought to go down to the seaside and have a rest for a few days. I've seen her employer, and he'll raise no objections. We'll have her closely watched, there might be another attempt on her life. And I thought we might make a little departure from the usual procedure then."

"How?"

"My friend Lessing could help, and if he stayed at the same hotel as the girl—"

"Not at all sure he could do anything of the kind," grumbled Chatworth. "One day he'll get into serious trouble. Still, can't stop him from staying at any hotel he likes, can we? Please yourself. But do you think you're much farther on? This organisation – any idea who is behind it?"

"None. It's probably to do with food, though. Food prices being as high as they are, thieves can make a fortune out of a single lorry-load of bacon and tinned goods. I can't help feeling that Randall stumbled across something which might have to do with Perriman's."

Chatworth grunted again.

"I can't make up my mind about Jeremiah Scott," Roger went on, "but I'm having a very careful watch kept on him. He has several food manufacturing companies on his list of clients. He'd be in an excellent position to go into factories and warehouses, make mental notes, put 'em down on paper as sketches as soon as he's alone, and then have them drawn up properly afterwards. Can't rule him out. If his story's true, he'd never heard of Kent Street until that day when he got the SOS from his brother, but ..." He shrugged his shoulders. "Odd little things keep worrying me, sir. He's a member of the Fulham Football Club, and there were those three programmes at the house."

"Nothing really odd about that, surely," said Chatworth. "Even I go to see football matches! Nothing else?"

"Nothing except routine," said Roger. "At the moment, the only line which might give results is Tommy Clayton, and I've a nasty feeling we might come across his body soon. Oh, there is a line I want to follow – I can't get it out of my head that Perriman's are the key to this business. They've a virtual monopoly of some foods. I propose to send Peel to look round their Woodhall factories."

"Then they'll know you're on to them."

"No, sir. Peel will take a job there. They're always advertising for warehousemen and labourers."

"Better Peel than your friend Lessing," growled Chatworth.

Roger went back to his office, to be told that a man was waiting downstairs to see him – a Mr Wilson. Wilson's card was on the desk, and Roger read:

James Wilson, Director
Crown Printing & Manufacturing Co. Ltd.

That had been Randall's firm. He telephoned for the caller to be brought up, and was soon greeting an athletic-looking, rather rugged young man with hair that was nearly ginger, a pair of alert, green-grey eyes, and a firm handclasp. Wilson was a little nervous, like many people who came to the Yard.

"Sit down," invited Roger, and pushed a box of cigarettes across the desk.

"I'll smoke a pipe, if I may," said Wilson, sitting down. "Understand you're now OC of the Randall case."

"I'm looking into it, yes," said Roger.

"Glad someone is. Guy Randall was a good chap – close friend of mine too. Made any progress?"

"These things take time," said Roger evasively.

"I suppose so. Happened to be in London today, visiting our office. The manager tells me you've seen him. Just want to say this: if we can help in any way, we will."

"Thanks very much," said Roger. "Have you any ideas about it, Mr Wilson?"

"Well—well, no," said Wilson. "Happiest chap alive. Engaged, all that kind of thing. Er—I wonder if you've any news about his fiancée? I mean, she isn't stranded or anything like that? Glad to help, if so."

"I think she's managing very well," said Roger reassuringly.

He went downstairs with Wilson, and watched him get into a gleaming Alvis and drive off.

Like that of Tucktos, the biggest Perriman factory was in an outer suburb of London – Woodhall. Unlike Tucktos, it was modern. The main building was tall, white-fronted and a railway siding, which was continually busy, was on the right of it. So was the huge garage shed, with its dozens of Perriman's big, smart vans with 'Mr and Mrs Perriman' painted on both sides. These and their trailers were always being serviced, while others waited at the loading platforms of the great warehouses. Perriman's, with over two thousand multiple stores throughout the country and a great wholesale business, was invariably busy. Practically everything sold in Perriman shops and wrapped in Perriman packets was manufactured here – jam, biscuits, cocoa, different proprietary goods, soups – an almost endless variety.

Peel discovered this when he had been working in the General Warehouse for two days. He was one of thirty male workers in the General Warehouse, a huge, five-storey building which housed all the small-packet goods – everything in two-pound containers or less.

Row after row of store bins and shelves met his gaze when he was taken round the floor on which he worked.

The foreman of Peel's floor was a little man named Ramsay, who had an artificial leg and walked slowly about his domain. He had been with the firm for thirty years and had watched it grow. He liked new workers to take an interest.

Peel was particularly interested in the transport arrangements, and spent some time at the main dispatch platform, where vans were being loaded. He discovered that a carefully worked out schedule of deliveries was planned, and that there was a Control Room in the Dispatch Department, run rather on the lines of the RAF or Naval Control Room. On duty day and night were several clerks who could tell the position of the fleet of vans – nearly four hundred strong – all over the country. If there was a breakdown or any kind of trouble, the van-driver telephoned Control and reported, and relief was arranged immediately.

Peel's main job was to help load electric trolleys which fed the Dispatch Department, and so he went between the General Warehouse and Dispatch a dozen times a day. He discovered and reported that it would be possible for a big raid to be made on the vans almost any night. Many were loaded overnight, sometimes by a night-shift, and started off soon after six in the morning. The loaded vans were near a side exit which led to the main road, and were always pointing towards the road so that they could be driven off quickly, and empty vans brought in for loading. There were two night-watchmen in this department, as well as the night Control Room staff, but as far as Peel could discover, no special precautions were taken.

Clad in a khaki overall and wearing a cloth cap, Peel loaded a trolley and gave the driver the all-clear. The trolley moved off silently down the wide gangway with bins on either side. Peel yawned. It was nearly four o'clock in the afternoon, and he had been up most of the previous night.

"Oi—Peel!" That was little Ramsay.

"Coming!" Peel walked along to the foreman's desk in the centre of the floor.

"Been over to the dump yet?" asked Ramsay.

"Dump? No, I haven't heard about it."

"Then it's time you did," said Ramsay. "Benny's hurt his foot, so I want you to take his barrow to the dump and burn the muck. Can't miss the dump, you can see the smoke over it all the time."

"Oh, I know it," said Peel.

Benny was an old labourer who swept the passages, collected the rubbish, sorted salvage, and took the real waste to an incinerator – or 'dump.' His wheelbarrow was already full, and Peel took it to the lift, which promptly delivered him to the ground floor near the main trading platform. The dump was between that and the railway siding.

A five-foot brick wall surrounded the heap of smouldering rubbish, and there was only one gap in the wall. Peel walked towards it over a cement path; his rubber-tyred barrow moved freely and quietly.

He wrinkled his nose because of the burning smell; there was something unusual about it.

Inside the wall was a big, round, uneven dump, like a small slag-heap. Flames licked here and there, but most of the rubbish was now smouldering ash. Spades, shovels, long-handled two-pronged forks and some axes were fastened in brackets to the rough brick wall.

One or two fresh piles of rubbish had recently been dumped, and Peel turned his own over near one of them. He picked up a long fork, and turned over some of the 'new' rubbish to try to start it blazing, and after a while his efforts made a merry little fire. But in turning the heap, he had made an evil-smelling smoke rise ... and there was a curious, sweetish odour which he thought he recognised – the smell of burning flesh. He told himself that he was crazy, that it was something from the factory which had been mixed with the rubbish.

The smell persisted and seemed to get stronger. He plunged the fork in again and again, without quite knowing what he expected to find but disliking the smell intensely. Then the fork caught in something, and he pulled out a piece of cloth, covered with black ash! He drew it nearer; it wasn't just a piece of cloth, it was part of a coat. The skirt and arms had been badly burned and charred, but the lapels, shoulders, and the top of the sleeves were easily recognisable when he spread it out on the ground. It had been folded, and where the creases had come it wasn't so dirty. When he saw the pattern, it was as if an electric shock had run through him.

This was a check coat – a large check pattern, like Tommy Clayton's.

Peel straightened up, took a firmer grip on the fork, and prodded and probed again. It wasn't long before the prongs were driven into something which yielded but from which he couldn't draw the fork easily. He left it in, picked up a short-handled spade and, regardless of the mess to his shoes and trousers, cleared the muck away.

He found a hand.

Chapter Sixteen

The Body in the Dump

Peel's stomach heaved. He cleared away more of the muck, and the arm was disclosed – badly burned, in places to the bone.

The arm moved easily.

It wasn't attached to the body.

Peel looked round. No one was in sight nearby, no one could see him working, except people in the upper floors of the buildings, and he was too far away to be identified. He wanted to run off, telephone the local police and get a squad out here, but he had to find out more about this.

He found a leg; that wasn't attached to the body, either.

Then he found the head.

He turned away suddenly, nausea overcoming him, and was violently sick. When that was over, he took out a cigarette and lit it with shaky fingers. Better report what he had found to the manager. If he went straight to the police, he would give himself away. His legs weren't very steady at first, but he threw off the effects of the discovery as he neared the gap in the wall. Now he could see a van-driver standing by the cabin of his vehicle, and several other workers.

He left the dump.

As he did so, he felt something touch his legs, looked down – and was thrown heavily to the ground. The 'something' was a piece of wire, with a hooked end, which had caught him round the ankle. He heard nothing, but the fall winded him.

Then he saw the man.

He caught only a glimpse of him – a man with a handkerchief tied round his face and a hat pulled over his eyes – and with a long shovel in his right hand. The shovel was raised, Peel sensed what was intended and twisted himself to one side. The blow caught him on the shoulder, his arm went numb and useless. He tried to shout, but the sound wasn't loud. He kicked at the fellow's legs, struck home and gave himself a moment's respite. The shovel came again – if the corner struck his head it would split his skull. He dodged; the thing clanged noisily on the cement path, and something hit his ear. Then he heard a shout from some way off …

Next moment a blow struck him behind the ear, and he fell flat again.

He held his breath, expecting the final killing blow – and then felt someone touch his shoulders and heard a man say: "Okay, mate, okay; take it easy!"

Peel sat up slowly.

"Now take it easy," the man said urgently. He was a stocky little fellow, peering closely into Peel's eyes. "You're okay – take it easy. Don't try to get up, just sit back a minute. They're fetching you a pick-me-up. You're okay."

Peel licked his lips.

"That—man—"

"They're after him, you're okay."

Two other men came out, and one of them had a flask of whisky. A new, authoritative voice spoke.

"Don't give him that, it'll go to his head. Let me have a look at him."

The newcomer was a small, middle-aged man, well-dressed, obviously a manager or one of the office staff. Peel sat obediently while the other examined his head, and it felt tender but not particularly painful. The man stepped back.

"Only a graze; perhaps a drink will do him good," he conceded.

The whisky trickled down Peel's throat, biting, welcome. He tried to stand up on his own, but couldn't; the others helped him up. He stared over the wall. Three men, all van-drivers, were coming away from the railway sidings, talking to one another.

"Did they get him?" Peel muttered.

"No," said the well-dressed man. "But the police will – don't worry about that." He frowned. "What was it all about?"

Peel told him.

If the local police were puzzled by Scotland Yard's prompt interest in the body in the dump, they didn't say so but welcomed Roger. A sergeant and a police-surgeon had arrived almost immediately. Seven or eight uniformed men were poking about the dump, the remains of the victim were placed side by side near the wall. Only a hand remained to be found – an arm with a badly charred and broken wrist had just come to light. So had the remnants of a pair of flannel trousers and two brown shoes, which had been surprisingly little damaged; there was even a trace of the printing inside the heel of the shoe, visible to the naked eye. It would be fairly easy to identify the clothes, although it would be a long time before the body itself could be identified.

Roger and the police-surgeon studied it.

"Youngish chap," the police-surgeon said. "Height about five seven or eight, I'd say. You'll trace him through his dentist, I expect. Can't think of any other way."

"Any idea how long he's been here?" asked Roger.

"Hard to say. Know who you want, don't you? Fire expert. Tell you more about it than I can," said the police-surgeon. "When your photographers have finished, I'd send the remains to the Yard, if I were you. No point in leaving them somewhere locally, and I can get a dentist working at them early in the morning."

"Tonight, please," asked Roger.

"All right, all right," grumbled the other.

Roger had a word with the local superintendent, whose men were still searching the smouldering rubbish, then turned towards the main factory buildings. As he drew near the platform, against which a dozen vans were backed, a man came out of a large office – a rather short, well-dressed man, accompanied by a foreman.

The well-dressed man saw Roger.

He drew back, knocking against his companion. It was a moment of shock, astonishment, alarm, and it seemed to Roger there was something else in his expression: fear. He didn't move, even when the foreman spoke to him, and Roger vaulted up to the platform level. The colour was drained from the man's face, and his hands were shaking.

"Mr Akerman – what's up, sir?" That was the foreman.

Akerman pulled himself together and approached Roger.

"Who—who are you?" he asked, and his voice quivered a little.

"Chief Inspector West of New Scotland Yard," Roger said brusquely. "Reason to be alarmed, sir?"

"Al—alarmed? Well, yes, in a way. It's incredible. You're the living image of him. You—but, of course, you know about him. I'm talking of Guy Randall."

"Yes, I know about Randall," said Roger heavily. He couldn't make up his mind whether the likeness was the full explanation of Akerman's manner. "Nasty business here, sir. Are you the—a manager?"

Akerman said: "Not here, I'm from the London offices. Francis Akerman, from the Buying Department. Er—yes, today's is another nasty business. I'm glad the local police haven't delayed sending for the Yard, we shall want to get to the bottom of it quickly."

Roger said: "I hope we shall. Who is in charge?"

"Mr Emanuel," said Akerman, and added hastily: "Mr Emanuel Perriman, that is – our managing-director. He will see you himself, I'm sure."

"Thanks," said Roger, "but I meant in charge of this department. I want to see the men who saw the attack on your warehouseman, please – what's his name? Peel, I think."

"The drivers have already been interviewed by the police," complained Akerman.

"They're still here, sir," said the foreman.

"Oh, are they? Good. You look after the Chief Inspector, and I'll tell Mr Emanuel that he's here."

Roger interviewed the van-drivers. None of them could describe Peel's assailant, except to say that he had been dressed in dark-brown and wore a handkerchief mask. During these interviews the foreman was present, and Roger asked him if any of the regular workers were missing.

"I couldn't say – it's been such a messy afternoon," said the foreman. "Tell you what might help, though – the time-cards."

"How can they help?"

"Well, if it's one of our staff, and that's what you obviously think, he wouldn't have clocked out, would he? The attacker just made off."

"He could have slipped in at another entrance and clocked out," said Roger. "But I'd like to find out who hasn't."

"Come along with me," said the foreman.

He led the way to the time-keeping office, outside which were racks of cards. Most of the cards were in one large rack, but there were a dozen in another – and the foreman told him these people hadn't clocked out; he himself was included. He ran through the names. Six were of women, who were working overtime in the wrapping shed. His made seven. He read out the other names aloud, and looked round the big shed, saying: "Danny's here ... Bob ... Tim ... Benny ... h'mm, Relf, he—"

"Who?" exclaimed Roger.

"Relf – one of the porters, and he's usually off on the tick," said the foreman with a sniff. "Name's familiar, is it?"

"It is rather. What's this Relf like?"

"Big powerful chap. Can't say I like him. General porter – odd-job man. He—"

The foreman broke off.

"Yes," encouraged Roger.

"He does more work on the dump than anyone else."

Roger said quietly: "I'll check up on Relf. None of the staff is missing, I suppose, apart from him?"

"No, no one. Why?"

"There *is* a corpse," Roger reminded him.

"Yes, yes. But it isn't one of our men, I'm sure."

"Noticed any strangers about here lately?" asked Roger.

The foreman said: "Well, there are always a few. Scrap merchants come up to see if we've anything for disposal. But—can't say—wait a minute, though. There was one fellow who's been more persistent than most of them. He *said* he was a scrap disposal merchant, and wanted to make an offer for everything we had. Been hanging about part of each day for the last week."

"What was he like?"

"Not a bad chap. About medium height, I suppose, or a bit less; rather plump. Had dark hair, and always wore the same clothes."

"And what were they like?"

"A black-and-white check sports coat and a pair of flannel trousers," said the foreman, and licked his lips again. "They—they found a black-and-white coat on the dump, didn't they? Or what was left of it."

Chapter Seventeen

Night Journeys

Everything pointed to the dead man being the newspaperman Clayton. And everything pointed to the missing Relf as Peel's assailant, for one of the railwaymen in the siding said that he had seen Relf run away from the factory and get on a motorcycle. Relf's address proved to be a rooming-house in the East End of London, and he wasn't there when the police called. Roger arranged for the house to be watched and for Relf's description to be circulated throughout the country. Then Akerman came for him – and with Akerman was Randall's friend, Wilson.

"Second meeting," Wilson said briefly. "I'm sorry about this – is it the same business?"

"It could be," said Roger.

"We've just been talking about it," said Akerman. "Mr Wilson has come to see the conditions in which our goods are wrapped and stored; it will give him a clearer idea of the requirements for our containers."

"I mean to do a good job for Randall's order," said Wilson.

Roger nodded.

"But you mustn't keep Mr Emanuel waiting," said Akerman.

Roger wasn't yet accustomed to the Perriman habit of calling their 'family members' by their Christian names, to distinguish one from another. There were Emanuel, Silas, and Matthew at Woodhall; Samuel and Joseph in London and a number of lesser Perrimans, the younger generation with more modern names. Mr Emanuel was the patriarch of the family which had established Perriman's first retail shop fifty-one years ago. He received Roger in a small, cosy office. He had a mop of thick white hair which waved back from his forehead, a bushy moustache, red, healthy cheeks, and clear blue eyes.

He was distressed by what had happened. He wanted the police to understand that every facility would be granted to help them in their inquiries. The name of Perriman was an honoured one, almost a revered one, in commerce; such a scandal as this, such an unhappy event, would smear that good name. If in the event it proved that a member of the staff of Perriman's was involved, then the police could be sure that it would shock everyone concerned.

A polite secretary led Roger out of the *sanctum sanctorum*.

By then an officer of the National Fire Service had arrived and was waiting near the dump for Roger. He said that there was a top layer of accumulated ash and debris which had been there, slowly increasing, for some weeks. In one part of the heap, however, there was evidence that this top layer had been removed and thrown to another place, and that a hole had been dug and filled with highly inflammable material. He suggested that the body had been put on top and the flames started. The blaze would be fairly brief – perhaps at its height for half an hour or so. The body would be badly burnt, enough to make it unrecognisable. Then it had been dismembered and dug in, and the top layer of ash and debris spread over it.

"What about the clothes?" asked Roger.

"He wasn't wearing the coat or the trousers," said the fire-expert.

The sifting of the dump would take all night and part of next day, but Roger was anxious to get it done as quickly as possible, and as anxious to stay on the spot as long as he could. The dispatch foreman stayed late and was a mine of information – he told Roger one thing which he hadn't learned from Peel's report. Twice a week, night journeys started from the factory. These were the middle-distance deliveries of goods to branches which could be reached after an all-night drive, so that the unloading could be done at the shops early next morning. About seventy vans were involved, and the journeys were made every Monday and every Thursday.

Tonight was Thursday.

Most of the vans were already loaded.

The journeys started at half-past eight, when the drivers and their mates gathered in the department, took their loading sheets and delivery notes and clocked out. Thirty seconds were allowed between the departure of each van; so the seventy were off in half an hour and five minutes – and at five past nine precisely, when it was dark outside, the last van rumbled off. Its driver was a lanky, cheerful fellow, and his mate a little Scotsman.

The last van out, as it happened, was the first to be held up.

Lanky Tim Holloway not only looked cheerful; he was an optimist by nature. Sandy McKay, sitting beside him, was of a dour and glum disposition. They were on a quiet stretch of road near Basingstoke when suddenly a figure loomed up in the headlights, a man who held his arms high above his head, and waved vigorously.

"Dinna take any risks," said Sandy quickly. "'Tis against ordis to give lifts, Lanky."

"Never said I was going to give no one a lift, did I?" demanded Lanky. "Like me ter run him over, would yer?" He pulled up slowly, and the headlights shone on a figure huddled up in the road. "Lumme! Someone been 'urt."

"I dinna like it," muttered Sandy. "There's been a lot of hold-ups, Lanky. Swerve, mon, and—"

But it was too late; Lanky had stopped just in front of the man who was lying in the road. The other man hurried to the cabin door. Lanky opened it and said: "Wot's up, mate?"

"Just put your hands up, chum," said the man by the door.

In the reflected light from the headlamps a gun showed clearly in his hand. Lanky gasped, Sandy swore. The 'victim' scrambled to his feet as Lanky and the Scotsman put up their hands.

"Now listen," said Lanky earnestly if nervously. "You won't come to no good doing a thing like this, mate."

The 'victim' had opened Sandy's door, and now stood back and ordered him to get out. Lanky was forced to climb down on the other side, and the man with the gun took them to the back of the van. The bar across the double doors was lowered and the doors opened, and the crew was made to climb inside. The armed man followed them. He hung a small, electric lamp on a nail on the side of the van, and sat on a carton of porridge oats. Lanky squatted on a side of bacon, and Sandy stood swaying from side to side, glowering in the gloom. The big van rolled slightly, and Lanky's face began to work. Once they lurched heavily, throwing Sandy into their captor and making him bang his head against the side. For a split second the man's attention was diverted and Sandy made a dive at him.

The man raised his right leg and kicked Sandy viciously in the groin. The little Scotsman squealed and sprawled over some cartons and fell, with cartons tumbling about him. He bent double, his breath coming in panting gasps.

The gun pointed straight at Lanky.

"Don't try any tricks," the hold-up man said.

His face was coated with grease-paint and he wore a big false moustache. His hat was pulled low over his eyes. The van swung towards the off side, and Lanky glanced about him nervously; then the van swung left – the driver had been swinging out to turn. They travelled along a rough road and then the van slowed down; stopped.

The gunman said, "Now get cracking. We want the bacon and bottled and canned fruits and jams. Bring it to the back of the van."

Sandy gasped: "I wouldna help ye if—"

The gunman leaned forward and struck him across the face with the barrel of his gun. Lanky made an ineffectual swing at him, which wasn't noticed. The door swung open, and the gunman jumped down and was joined by the driver. They lowered the tailboard with a crash, then put up the chains to make it secure. Under the threat of the gun, Lanky and the Scotsman, his face bleeding, shifted the food.

Another man joined the two outside. They lifted the cases, packages, and sides of bacon out of sight. At last the job was finished.

Lanky wiped the sweat off his forehead. Behind him, the van looked a shambles of cartons, split packages, and powders. There was a half-case of jam, most of the glass jars of which had been broken – the red jam spread over the floor like thick blood.

One of the hold-up men stood by the tailboard with his gun. Another jumped aboard and a cosh appeared in his hand. He raised it and the shiny leather glinted. Lanky struck at his hand but missed, and the cosh descended on his temple, knocking him sideways. It fell again on the nape of his neck, and he pitched forward, unconscious.

Sandy flung a jar of jam at his assailant.

The man dodged; the jam-jar smashed, another sticky mess appeared on the wall. The man with the cosh struck savagely – struck again when Sandy was unconscious, struck a third time until the man with the gun ordered: "Stop it – now get down."

The assailant kicked Sandy's unconscious figure, and then obeyed. The couple put up the tailboard, shut the doors and dropped the bar into position. Then they hurried to a small van, which was in front of the Perriman one, climbed in beside the driver who was already at the wheel, and drove off.

Eleven other vans were held up in much the same way; the same kind of food was taken.

The chief clerk of the Control Room was sitting at his desk, working on a mass of figures. It was four o'clock. His assistant was drawing on a big map, planning Monday's schedules. What a life! Always the same! No excitement, not much fun. What a life! He ...

Brrr-brrr! Brrr-brrr!

That was the telephone nearest him.

His assistant looked up.

"I'll answer," said the chief clerk, and took off the receiver. "Perriman's Control Room."

"Hold on, I'll put you through," a girl said.

"*Percy!*" A hoarse voice sounded on the line, and the clerk sensed the speaker's tension.

"Who's speaking?" he demanded.

"It's Lanky – Percy, listen. We bin 'eld up. Mac's been knocked abaht somefink awful. I'm at an AA box, forced me aht of the lorry. I sent for the police. I'm near Basingstoke …"

The Wests were early risers; less by inclination, especially when Roger had been out late, than because the boys disturbed the morning peace from about seven o'clock. Or rather, Scoopy did – he was always the chief culprit. Roger, lying in his own bed, opened his eyes and saw sunlight flooding a corner of the room and heard Scoopy reciting in a sing-song voice, a dirge-like tune:

"Half a pound of tup'ney rice,
 Half a pound of treacle.
 That's the way the money goes,
 Pop goes the weazel!"

Roger grinned.

Janet, next to him, for Nell Goodwin had insisted on sleeping in the dining-room that night, was facing the window, and appeared to be fast asleep.

Roger got up and went to Scoopy's room – and as soon as he opened the door the singing stopped. Scoopy was sitting up in bed and wearing his dressing-gown.

"Good morning, Daddy!"

"Morning, old chap. Pipe down, will you? Mummy's very tired and Richard's still asleep. I'll bring your orange juice in a minute."

"Could *I* come and help you, Daddy?"

"Well, all right – but put your slippers on."

"They *are* on," declared Scoopy, and scrambled out of bed, wearing a gay pair of felt slippers. They went downstairs, the child chattering, and as they reached the hall Richard called out in a sleepy voice: "S'oopy! I'se awake."

Roger made the tea and prepared orange juice for the boys. Richard was already on the landing, his dressing-gown on but unfastened, one sash dragging on the floor, his slippers in his hand, his great eyes heavy with sleep. He was much slighter than Scoopy, and at first glance the more attractive. Scoopy was his idol.

"Now put those slippers on," began Roger, "and—"

The telephone rang, bringing the news of the night's raids.

Chapter Eighteen

Headlines

The foreman of the Dispatch Department looked badly shaken when Roger arrived at Perriman's just after half-past nine. But he was on top of his job. He had reports of all the hold-ups, which coincided with provincial police-reports which Roger had collected from the Yard. The only man badly hurt was Sandy McKay, and he was in hospital with a smashed rib, caused by a kick. His head injuries weren't serious. A number of the other drivers and vanmen had been slightly hurt when resisting; all the robberies had been completely successful.

The foreman had prepared a total of goods lost.

"Worst we've ever had," he said. "It's awful."

"How often have you had trouble before?" Roger demanded.

The foreman cited at least a dozen robberies.

"I'd like to get this clear," Roger said quietly. "There's a regular schedule of journeys, and a copy of each schedule goes to various departments. On the schedule there's an hour-by-hour statement of where the vans ought to be – an estimated log. Right?"

The foreman nodded.

"And if a man got hold of a copy of that log, he'd pretty well know where to find the vans," Roger commented. "When are the schedules prepared?"

"Saturday for Monday's journeys, Wednesday for Thursdays," said the foreman. "Here's one."

He took down a large pink folder which, when opened out, covered most of his desk. Printed on it were the names of branches within a hundred-mile radius of London – others within a two-hundred-mile radius. Beneath each branch was printed *'Regular Weekly'* and, in ink, additional 'special' items requested by the branch were entered. On the reverse side were details of the vans which were doing the various journeys, and the estimated time of arrival at certain points along the road and at the branches.

Roger glanced at the foot of the sheet, and saw the words:

'Printed by Tucktos Ltd, London, NW.'

"Who has copies?" Roger asked.

"Branch Sales Department, Central Warehouse, General Office, Secretaries' Office, London HQ, and two stay down here," said the foreman. "This is one for last night."

"The sheet and regular orders are printed in quantities, and the other details are filled in by ink, then?" Roger said.

"Yes." The man looked on a shelf on which were a number of ledgers and papers, and took down some of the folders. He glanced at them quickly and put them aside. Then he looked at Roger in bewilderment.

"The other one's missing," he said worriedly.

"When did you last see it?"

"Well, yesterday some time," said the foreman. "They're always on that shelf."

"Did Relf ever come into the office?" demanded Roger.

"Yes, to sweep up," said the foreman. "I've seen him messing about these shelves too, and gave him a piece of my mind. I never did like that fellow."

"Would the buying office in London have access to one of these sheets before the deliveries?" asked Roger.

"Not a prepared one, that goes to London later. They get the printing done, of course."

"So they know about the schedules?"

"Oh yes. And Mr Samuel or Mr Akerman might have access to one, if it comes to that – any one of the bosses."

"Anyone ever come here to examine them?" asked Roger.

The foreman rubbed his chin.

"Well, yes, sometimes, but no one from London; this doesn't affect the London people much. They're fairly new – only started them in this form seven months ago; used to have a book. I had a hectic day going through the books and drawing up the lists! Chap from the printers was here with me part of the time – nice chap," added the foreman. "We happened to mention football, and he's a Fulham supporter, like me."

"Oh," said Roger, as if casually. "I go along to the Cottage occasionally too. Now, I'll want one of these journey-sheets as a sample – an old one or an unused one will do."

Every van-driver and assistant was questioned that day, and pressed to describe the assailants. One or two vague descriptions were forthcoming, but most of the hold-up men had been disguised or had worn masks. Relf didn't return to his lodgings, but the police discovered where he had spent his evenings, what friends he had, and went on probing. He was the other Relf's brother.

Obviously the overall plan was only now beginning to unfold; Randall's murder had brought it to light. This was food robbery in a big way, so there must be ready outlets for the stolen food. Find it, and they'd be on their way to solving the case.

A small hoard of bacon was found in one shop; it was the same cure as others found elsewhere, and the Perriman chemists stated without hesitation that it was a Perriman product. Canned goods, although their labels had been taken off them, were found to come from Perriman's.

Within twenty-four hours of the robberies much of the goods had been found in small shops all over the country, whose owners were prepared to buy cheap with no questions asked, and to restaurants and cafés. Stolen Perriman goods were marketed as far north as Carlisle, and as far south as Bournemouth and Brighton.

It was on the day after the discovery of the body in the dump that the newspapers began to storm about the outbreak of food hold-ups. They had been fully reported in all the Press on the following day, but the *Echo,* with a dozen provincial dailies in the same chain of newspapers, now came out with startling front-page headlines – and they all said virtually the same thing.

Roger read the *Echo* at his desk at the Yard.

FOOD THIEVES MURDER *ECHO* REPORTER; POLICE INQUIRIES FAIL

'It is believed by the police and by this newspaper that the body of a man found on a rubbish dump at Perriman's factory at Woodhall was that of the renowned *Echo* reporter, Thomas Clayton, whose sensational articles dealing with all aspects of crime are known to all our readers. The body was horribly mutilated and partly burnt. The *Echo* believes that Clayton's investigations led him to Perriman's and that he had advance information about the series of crimes perpetrated on England's main roads two nights ago.

And Clayton was ahead of the police in this.

The *Echo* does not believe in belabouring the police. Scotland Yard has a mighty task, and on the whole performs it well. But there are features in this crime – one of a series of crimes – which we find disturbing. Twelve food vans were held up; at least thirty-six men were involved in these outrages; not one has been detained. As far as we know, little of the stolen foodstuff has been recovered. The scoop was sensational, and police inquiries have been foiled.

It would not have been worthwhile but for the scandalously high price of food.

The *Echo* therefore urges the Government to institute an official inquiry into food prices, food monopolies, and food distribution and supports Sir Elias Perriman in his demand for this in the House of Commons.

We again tell the Government that their dear food policy is creating not only hardship to millions but also the odious crimes which are the result of it.

Eddie Day looked up from his desk.

"Bit hot, aren't they?" he remarked.

"Can't blame them," said Roger, "although we don't know that the body was Clayton's."

"Only want proof," sniffed Eddie.

"Useful thing for us to have," said Roger with a grin. He telephoned the police-surgeon's office – speaking to the man who had first seen the charred body. "It's West here – anything fresh about the body in the dump, or aren't you worrying about it?"

"Needn't be sarcastic," growled the police-surgeon. "As a matter of fact, we've got Clayton's dentist coming out this afternoon. He's been down with 'flu, couldn't come before. Want to see him?"

"Yes, please," said Roger. "What time?"

"Half-past two," said the police-surgeon.

Roger watched Clayton's dentist poking about inside the mouth of the dead man, peering through a tiny magnifying-glass with the help of a small electric torch, and disliked this more than most *post-mortems*.

"Whoever it was, it wasn't Clayton," the dentist said at last. "This mouth has different fillings from those I use. Clayton may be dead, but this isn't him."

Roger said: "Thanks. Now we want to find the dentist who actually did that work; then we might find out who the victim was."

Back in his own office, he first telephoned the *Echo* and told them to stop running the story that it was Clayton's body; then he telephoned Mrs Clayton.

He had hardly replaced the receiver when the telephone rang. A superintendent of the East End Division was on the line, a terse, laconical man.

"West?"

"Yes?"

"I think we can put our hands on your man Relf," said the superintendent. "At an old warehouse near the docks. We were looking for stolen foods, and heard this chap had been seen to go into the warehouse on the night that Peel was attacked. Arrived on a motorcycle that someone else drove off. Coming over?"

"Am I! Done anything yet?"

"I've got the place surrounded," said the superintendent. "Any chance of getting the AC to authorise guns, d'you think?"

"I do," said Roger.

Half an hour later he reached the docks, with two sergeants and three DOs; each man carried a revolver, and Roger had a spare one for the superintendent, a bulky, pale-faced man wearing a bowler hat, who was standing at a corner of a narrow street leading to the docks when the Yard car drew up. Roger got out, and saw that half a dozen Divisional men were about.

"Any move?" he asked.

"Not yet – no one's come out or gone in." He pointed to a raggedly dressed man with unkempt hair who stood miserably between two uniformed policemen. "He squeaked," he said.

Roger approached the man.

He had dirty skin, broken teeth, bleary eyes and a whining voice. He knew Relf – slightly, just as he'd known Relf's brother. Used to help at the garage, that's how. He'd seen a man he thought was Relf drive up on a motorcycle on the evening in question, and go inside; someone else had come out and driven the motorcycle off. The warehouse was supposed to be empty, but he'd seen other men go in and come out, always after dark.

"Where's the warehouse?" Roger asked the superintendent.

"Can't see it from here – we've only covered the approaches so far," said the other. "We've got it under surveillance from the windows of a rubber warehouse next door."

Five minutes' walk took them to a huge, grey building, not far from the docks. They could see the tops of the ships that were being unloaded, hear the occasional hoot of a tug's siren, the clatter of cranes and machinery.

Outside the grey-walled warehouse there was a curious, heavy smell – not the smell of manufactured rubber, something different, rather overpowering and choking. Inside, bales of rubber were piled up from floor to ceiling. The Divisional police had made the necessary arrangements with the foreman, and Roger, the superintendent, and a Yard sergeant named Coker entered the warehouse, watched by porters who trundled bales of rubber along on hand-trolleys.

They reached a lift, and were taken up to the fifth and top floor by a little lascar.

This floor was nearly empty – huge storerooms had only a few tons of rubber dotted about, but there were a lot of odd bales. Two of these were placed in front of a small window, and Roger stood on them and looked at the warehouse next door.

It was only a few yards away from this one – and was little more than a shell. The windows were blackened, and a part of the roof had caved in. It looked derelict and useless – and on either side were bombed-sites, piled up with rubble.

"What's the roof like over there?" asked Roger.

"Part of it's all right," said the superintendent. "So I'm told by the district surveyor, anyway. Going in from the top? If you ask me, we should wait until after dark."

"They've more chance of slipping through after dark," Roger said. Strictly speaking, this was the superintendent's responsibility, and he didn't want to insist. "I'll use my men, if you like."

"Like hell you will! Have wondered whether it's wise to wait myself. Don't worry about me, West; tell me what you want me to do, and I'll fix it."

"Thanks," said Roger. "You take a squad to the front entrance and send another to the side door. I'll tackle the roof with my chaps. We want some stout ladders to span it."

"Can do," said the superintendent.

Three-quarters of an hour later, strong ladders had been placed across the narrow gap between the two warehouses, and the police had ropes round their waists in case they slipped. It was about five o'clock, and the sun was warm and bright, although a great bank of clouds was in the south, sluggishly approaching London.

Roger led the way across the ladders.

He paused on the other roof, which was flat where it wasn't broken. A gaping hole showed on one side, but it looked as if most of the roof was sound, and on the sound part was a big roof-light, railed off and with the window shut.

Roger led the way to the roof-light.

He approached it carefully, and went down on one knee before he looked in. All he saw was an iron ladder leading down to a narrow passage. He stood back, and one of his men opened the light. Roger went down first.

The ladder was covered with dust, and when he stepped on the concrete below, he stirred up a great cloud. Immediately he wanted to sneeze. He stifled it as best he could, but men above started sneezing; they needed muslin masks to keep out the dust. He listened intently but heard no sounds from below, so at last he beckoned the others.

The passage led to a doorway, but there was no door. Beyond was a flight of wooden steps, and they walked softly, although nothing could prevent the boards from creaking. The dust and cobwebs convinced Roger that the upper floors hadn't been visited for a long time; if Relf's friends used the place, they stayed downstairs.

The staircase led to a huge, deserted chamber, with glassless windows and a musty smell. The next landing was a replica of the first, and there were three more. The first-floor landing was much cleaner. There were places where a broom had been drawn across the dust, and piles of dust were in the corners.

"Now we're getting somewhere," Roger said softly.

He slipped his right hand into his pocket; the unfamiliar feel of the gun was reassuring. He paused, and fancied that he heard a noise but couldn't be sure. The front doors of the warehouse were closed, but a window immediately above them let in some light.

He crept down the stairs to the ground floor, the five men in single file after him.

There was a basement below – cellars probably. But there was plenty to interest him here. Men had come in and out of the warehouse frequently; a regular path had been trodden through the thin coating of dust. He went to the big doors. A smaller one was set in one of them, and he examined the Yale-lock and the knob. There were traces of oil, and when he turned the knob, the barrel of the lock moved easily.

There were oily marks leading from the inset door to the stairs which went down into the basement – marks of a heel, a toe – sometimes just a smear. Obviously there was a patch of oil somewhere outside, and the men who used the warehouse trod on it every time they entered.

"One of you by the door," ordered Roger.

A detective-officer moved across, Roger and the others turned towards the basement.

Roger heard footsteps ringing out clearly on the stairs below, and then a man appeared, a little fellow with square shoulders, a wasp waist, a knotted scarf which was tied like a cravat, and a mop of greasy, black hair. The police hadn't time to dodge out of sight; the man saw them before he had reached the top of the stairs. His mouth opened and his eyes bulged, even before Roger snatched out his revolver.

"Keep still!" hissed Roger. "And keep quiet!"

The little crook stood gaping. One of the sergeants advanced a few paces, and as he did so a man out of sight called: "What's up, Percy?"

'Percy' made a curious, little, whistling noise in his throat – then turned and leapt down the stairs before anyone could stop him.

Chapter Nineteen

Hide-and-Seek

The sergeant nearest the stairs jumped forward as Roger glanced round at the man by the door and called: "Warn the men outside!"

The sergeant reached the top of the stairs as running footsteps sounded in the cellar, accompanied by raised voices – orders, Roger fancied. A door slammed. The sergeant slipped on the top step, and Roger grabbed him.

"There was a light," said the sergeant.

It was pitch-dark now until Roger took out a pencil-torch, and its narrow beam moved about the space, showing the bottom step, the dust, the concrete floor. Another man switched on a more powerful torch. They could not see the walls, for this was a huge chamber – and they could not be sure that it was empty. The door, presumably that which had been slammed, was immediately opposite the foot of the stairs, about thirty feet away from them.

"Try to find a light-switch," Roger said as he went quickly down the stone steps.

It struck cold.

Roger stood still, and the silence was broken by a sharp click of the switch. But no light came on.

From the ground-floor hallway, the superintendent called out in his deep voice: "All the roads covered outside. I'm coming down."

When he arrived, Roger and a sergeant were examining the lock of the door, and another man was walking round the walls. The lock of the one door was modern, and it looked as if it had been recently fitted.

"Steel door, painted over," said Roger. "Be quickest to get an oxyacetylene cutter."

While two men went for the cutter and equipment, Roger and the Divisional man made a quick tour of the nearby streets and alleys.

Two of the Divisional men stood at every corner.

"Satisfied?" asked the superintendent, when they came within sight of the entrance to the derelict warehouse again.

Roger nodded.

"No one could have covered the place better."

They entered the warehouse again and heard a hissing sound. From the top of the stairs they saw a goggled man on his knees in front of the door. The big cellar was filled with garish light, so bright that it dimmed the light from half a dozen oil-lamps which had been brought in and stood about the floor.

Already there were two straight cuts in the metal, near the lock, and the flame was cutting another line. Roger looked at it, sideways, keeping his eyes narrowed against the glare. Suddenly the flame swung away from the door and faded.

"Okay now," said the man.

A policeman stepped forward and pulled at the door. It opened slowly.

Roger called: "Be careful. Keep behind the door, they may try shooting."

But when the door stood open, nothing happened.

Roger stepped forward slowly, his gun raised.

The light behind him was enough to fill the entrance to the second room. There were no steps. The floor seemed polished. He knew that if anyone lurked inside, he would make a clear target, but someone had to go first. He passed through the doorway, with the superintendent and two others close behind him, and peered right and left. There were stacks of something which showed a pale, yellow blur on either side. He took another step forward ...

His heel skidded, his feet shot up, he fell heavily on his back, exclaiming aloud as he fell. He lost his hold on his gun, and as he hit the floor, it slipped from his fingers and slithered along. The superintendent came to help – and also slipped. Two other men skidded and crashed down, unable to help themselves. In the doorway, detectives stood staring in astonishment.

Roger tried to get up, but his feet and hands slipped; he fell again, this time forward; his head, his knees, and his nose hitting the floor. He kept quite still for a few seconds, then slowly raised himself to his knees, but felt them slipping on the greasy floor. His hands were already covered in grease. He could see the others in the same plight, trying to get up, cautiously, tensely.

Torches shone into the room, and some of the lamps were pushed into the doorways, so that they could see every corner. Against the walls were stacks of cheese, bacon, boxes of canned food, and a few crates of butter, one of which had been broken open.

Roger tried to get up again, but couldn't; he would have to crawl or slither away. The crooks had spread butter over the floor.

A new sound broke the scraping, slithering noises – something so unexpected that it made every man's head jerk up and every eye turned towards the corner from which it came. A man coughed.

Roger got up on his hands and knees cautiously and then crawled, an inch at a time, towards the piles of provisions. He could see that the greased stretch of floor ran right across the room, but was only about four feet wide, and that he would be able to stand upright beyond it.

The superintendent stopped near him.

"I'll teach 'em," he muttered.

Two detectives still stood in the doorway, wary of the greasy floor. Others arrived with heaps of dirty sacking, put some down near the door, and then advanced slowly, covering the whole of the greased area. This led to another door, opposite the first, and Roger retrieved his gun and went to have a look at it. This door wasn't steel.

"Need axes, do we?" asked the superintendent.

"Yes," said Roger. He looked at the corner from which the cough had come and it came again. Piles of cheeses were there, all wrapped in muslin cheese-cloths.

"Get those cheeses cleared," the superintendent said.

Men went gingerly towards the corner. Two came in with long-handled axes and began to smash at the door. Roger and the superintendent reached the cheeses.

It was easier to get a fair idea of the amount of foodstuffs stacked down here now. Certainly much more than the proceeds of the Perriman hold-ups – he estimated that there were twenty tons of bacon, several tons of cheese, thousands of cases of canned fruit and jam.

"I hope the *Echo* prints *this,*" said the superintendent sourly.

The cough came again, but it was farther away now. By then, most of the food had been cleared from the corner, and they could see a hatch with a broken glass top. There was only darkness beyond it – darkness and the fading coughing.

"I wish I knew where that leads to," said the superintendent.

Roger stepped forward – and as he reached the hatch a flash showed up in the darkness beyond. He dodged instinctively as the report followed, and he heard the bullet smack into a cheese. The men darted to one side.

"We've got 'em," the superintendent muttered.

Roger said slowly. "Maybe we've cornered them. We can't raid 'em as we are. Better have tear-gas – how long will it take you to get some?"

"Quarter of an hour." The superintendent gave the order in an undertone, and a man moved off.

"They *can't* get away," said the superintendent.

Roger said: "Let's hope not. I'm going to try talking to them." He raised his voice and called: "Ahoy, there!"

No answer came.

"Ahoy, there!"

Still no answer.

"You're only wasting your time," Roger called. "We'll get you. And if you hurt anyone with that pop-gun, you'll get ten years."

He might have been talking to himself.

"Be careful, you're getting too near," the superintendent warned.

"They'll try—"

A flash and – crack!

Another bullet had buried itself in the cheese.

A new sound came, quietly at first but with increasing volume – the sound of running footsteps. Then there was a shot, nowhere near the hatch, not aimed at the policemen; they couldn't even see the flash. Another shot, but the running footsteps came on. There was a man's harsh voice.

"Get him – get him!"

Roger went forward, but no shot came. The footsteps were nearer, and the shouting was much clearer. He heard the bark of a shot, not aimed at him but at the running man. He flung one leg over the hatch, touched the floor on the far side, drew the other leg through …

Crack!

This time the flash was so near that it illuminated two things – the man who had fired and the figure of a man running towards Roger but still twenty or thirty yards away. He caught only that glimpse, had no idea who was running – but he heard other footsteps close behind. He glanced round, saw the superintendent outlined against the hatch, crouching low as if he were about to climb in, and then a man swore and another shot rang out.

"Watch that hatch!" roared a man inside this chamber. "Don't let the dicks …"

His voice trailed off.

The running man had stopped, but Roger could hear his breathing. He could hear that of other men, too, on both sides of the hatch.

Did the crooks know that he, Roger, was here?

His hold on the gun tightened.

It was fairly light near the hatch, but the light soon faded and he could see only piles of boxes or crates, behind which all the crooks were hiding now.

He heard a stifled sneeze, followed at once by a flash which made everything seem bright, but caught only a glimpse of the man with the gun.

A man muttered: "They'll be using weepy-gas in a minute, we'd better scram."

The man they had first heard shouting said harshly: "We're going to get that swine before we go."

Footsteps sounded in the outer chamber; policemen were coming towards the hatch, probably with the tear-gas. Roger's only task now was to prevent the crooks from killing the fugitive.

He raised his gun.

The man out of sight fired, and the shot seemed much louder. The flame was a vivid yellow, and in it Roger saw the fugitive.

It was Clayton of the *Echo!*

Clayton gasped and drew back. Roger fired at the man with the gun, and the bullet struck a box. There was an exclamation of surprised alarm, an oath.

"All right, Clayton," Roger called softly. "Just hold on a few minutes."

Clayton didn't answer. "We got to scram," a man hissed.

"We're going to get Clayton," said the man with the harsh voice. "He knows a lot too much."

Something was tossed through the broken window and hit the floor, breaking with a little tinkling sound. The tear-gas. Roger grinned in his relief, then prepared to breathe in the gas.

There was a rustling movement behind him.

"That you, Clayton?" he asked softly.

There was no answer, but another phial of tear-gas broke and he could smell the acrid stuff. He took out his handkerchief and held it over his nose and mouth. A man began to cough, then others started, there was an end to silence. He heard shuffling footsteps; the crooks were getting out.

Something else came in at the hatch – and as it hit the floor it burst with a vivid, green flame, lighting up every part of this cellar – the dozens of packing-cases, the floor, the ceiling, Clayton who was crouching on his knees behind a case, three men who seemed to be a long way off, the clinging gas, billowing up now, the whiteness taking on a green tinge – Roger saw all that, but didn't see the man behind him.

He felt a heavy, painful blow, and the blackness of unconsciousness.

Chapter Twenty

Alone

There was a bright, flickering light in front of Roger's eyes, which caused a pain like the slash of a knife across his forehead. The back of his head was sore. He smoothed his forehead with the palm of his hand; the pain eased and the light grew steadier.

He opened his eyes wide for the first time, and looked about him. He was in a tiny compartment, with wooden walls, a dusty, concrete floor and a dirty ceiling. The light came from a naked electric lamp suspended above his head, and it was swaying slightly to and fro.

He was lying on the floor, on his side. He straightened up slowly, until he was sitting with his back to the wall with his legs stuck straight out in front of him. The effort of moving made the pain at the back of his head worse, and the sharp knife-like flashes across his forehead came more frequently.

His hands and feet weren't tied, and the door of the little cubicle was ajar. Was he in the cellar of the warehouse?

He stood up slowly.

The blood thumped through his head, and he leaned against the wall with his eyes closed until the pain eased. Then he moved away from the wall and stepped towards the door; every movement brought the blood flooding to his head again. How long had he been here? He glanced at the wrist-watch on his left wrist, and thought for the first time of Janet, who had given him the watch. Janet would soon be told that he was missing. It was nearly nine o'clock. And the watch was ticking. He must get a move on; open the door. Oh – his gun! He tapped his pocket, but it was gone.

He pulled open the door and stepped through into a passage. It was dark out here, the only light came from the room. He stood on the threshold, peering right and left, and heard rats scurrying. He tapped the floor with his toe; it was hard and smooth; more concrete. And it was cold down here.

Then he caught sight of some electric switches near the door, moved quickly, and pressed one down. Light came on some distance away along the passage. Great cobwebs hung from the ceiling and the walls, and everything seemed dirty. One of the walls was cemented, but the other was of brick – rough brick-work, with the mortar showing between the bricks and places where it had fallen out. The passage was narrow – about three feet wide. He heard a new sound.

At first it scared him, but he listened intently. It was a distant tapping noise, interspersed now and again with a loud boom. Men were trying to break through a wall – of course, that was it!

He moved cautiously towards the tapping sound and towards the light. They ought to get a pneumatic drill to force a way through the wall, that would get him out in no time.

The wall—*was* it a wall?—was a long way off.

Why hadn't the crooks killed him?

Silly question. Murder was seldom committed without a powerful motive; even these men would hesitate to kill for the sake of it. He had been knocked out to prevent him from helping Clayton, that was all.

This was a hell of a long passage.

He turned and looked over his shoulder, seeing the light coming from the cubicle at least fifty yards away.

The tapping was nearer. Perhaps he was—

There came something new – a fierce, wild roar, blasting the air with a stunning crash.

Explosion!

The ceiling and the floor moved darkly, as if they had been stirred up by a gigantic spade, and then he heard the roar of falling earth and bricks and stone – and felt the blast. It swept him off his feet and blew him yards along the passage. Not only him, but earth and bricks and dust, so that he was caught up in a fantastic maelstrom.

He was just aware of the tightness and difficulty of breathing, of being lifted off his feet. He was surrounded by dirt and dust, was struck a tattoo of blows on his back, his arms, and legs – he'd been turned round although he did not realise it.

He crashed down on to the floor and lay still. Debris fell about him, something cut his forehead. He couldn't see, gulped for breath, then began to cough. It was dark again.

The spasm of coughing ended, leaving him limp, weak, dazed, and not fully aware of the fact that he was breathing more easily now. He lay there for a long time, until the throbbing in his ears grew fainter and he was able to move his arms and legs. He tried to get up, but a heavy weight pressed on his back and legs. He managed to press his hands against the floor, to try to lever himself up with his arms; but couldn't manage it.

Something was pinning him down. His fingers went into something soft. It felt like pushing his fingers into the soil of the ground when he was planting in the garden.

The ceiling had come down and the earth above had been loosened. He was buried alive, and …

Then a second explosion came, something smashed on his head, he lost consciousness again.

Sir Guy Chatworth, big in sandy-coloured plus fours, wearing a bright-blue, pork-pie hat, stood by a hole which had been made in the wall of the warehouse cellar, nearly an hour before. There had been a small, steel door, with piles of rubble behind it, and making the hole had been easier than tackling the door. Sergeant Peel stood by his side, with the superintendent and half a dozen men who were resting on their spades and shovels. Beyond the hole men were working – shovels were striking bricks and stone as they made a narrow tunnel through the earth, but it was a slow business.

Peel was saying, "We were nearly through when we heard the explosion. The blast knocked half a dozen of us over, and it was some time before we were able to get working again."

Chatworth grunted.

Peel moistened his lips.

"No way of telling how much earth we've got to move. We've had an engineer in from the docks. We'll have to start carrying the rubble from the passage into here, so that there's room to move, and shore up the roof. There isn't room for more than one man at a time, with a shovel or spade – that's part of the trouble. And the engineer says he can't get a mechanical cutter into the confined space. We've got a team working and they're bringing some buckets so that we can shift the rubble."

Chatworth grunted again.

The superintendent said: "Can't be sure West's in there. Might have been taken out at the other exit."

Chatworth looked at him balefully. "Know your district, superintendent?"

"Every inch of it, sir."

"Then why can't you tell us where the other end of this tunnel comes out?" Chatworth went forward and looked through the hole in the wall. The men, working by the light of hurricane lamps, were stripped to the waist.

He turned away.

"Got maps of the vicinity?" he asked.

"Oh yes, sir," said the superintendent. "We've some at the station, but I've sent to the Town Hall to collect others from the surveyor's department. It's possible that this passage leads to another warehouse. Underground passages aren't unusual round here – some old sewers were converted after the main sewers were laid deeper."

Chatworth nodded and moved off, stepping gingerly over the sacking. He reached the door at the extreme end of the sacking, then suddenly turned round.

"Peel!" he called. "Peel!"

Peel went forward.

"Thought you were at Perriman's factory," said Chatworth.

"I am, by day, sir."

"What are you doing here?"

"I telephoned to report to Mr West, and learned what had happened, so I came straight over."

"Anything special to report?"

"I saw the man Scott – Jeremiah Scott – at the factory this afternoon. He was looking at some cartons in the warehouse, and I thought Mr West should know that he's obviously familiar with the warehouse and the Dispatch Department."

"Quite right. Jeremiah Scott, eh. How long have you been here?"

"About half an hour," said Peel. "Thought much about this?"

"I was wondering whether by any chance there is a Perriman's warehouse near here," said Peel.

"Same thought struck me," said Chatworth. "Check it, will you? I'm going to that café across the road to get a sandwich – missed my dinner. Come and have a snack when you've finished."

"Thank you very much, sir," said Peel.

He went to the public-house and borrowed the telephone directory, looked down the P's and came upon the imposing little section, in heavy black type, which covered the Perriman enterprises. The fifth out of nine addresses of the company was: 'Middleton Dock and Warehouse, Wapping.'

He went to Chatworth, and had hardly passed on the information before the superintendent and a middle-aged, sharp-featured man arrived, carrying large sheets of cardboard under their arms. Inside these were maps. Chatworth commandeered two tables in the café, and the sharp-featured man began to speak in a rather aloof voice, pointing with a long, tapering forefinger at different spots in the first map.

The derelict warehouse was marked with a red blob, and the stranger, who was from the surveyor's office at the Town Hall, said acidly: "This is where we are now. There's the river, these loops and whorls here show locks, quays, waterways – it's an irregular series, rather like an indented coast-line, although it's all built up. These here"—he pointed to a number of squares—"are the warehouses within a hundred yards radius."

Chatworth bit into his sandwich. "Tunnels?"

The forefinger stabbed again and traced thin, black lines.

"Known tunnels or underground passages here. There are plenty of them, as you can see. At one time a lot of the warehouses around here were owned by the same firm, but they split up and the tunnels were mostly walled-up – not all of them."

Chatworth said: "I see. Thanks."

"Where's Middleton Dock Warehouse?" asked Peel.

Chatworth looked at him sharply.

"Oh, Perriman's place," said the surveyor. He stabbed at the second sheet and indicated a square which was about two hundred and fifty yards from the derelict building.

"That's it. Biggest and most up-to-date on this part of the river. Any special reason for asking?"

"I'd heard it was a fine place," Peel murmured, and earned a covert glance of approval from Chatworth and a glare from the superintendent, who had no time for such irrelevancies.

Chatworth said to the surveyor: "That's very helpful of you – thank you very much, sir." The surveyor's severe expression thawed somewhat. "Where can we get you if we want you in a hurry?" Chatworth added.

"I'd like to go and have a look at the place where the trouble started," said the surveyor.

"Yes, yes, by all means." Chatworth waved the surveyor out of the café, and said: "Middleton's is really Perriman's, is it?"

"Yes, sir," said Peel.

'Middleton's' was surrounded by a ten-foot wall, but the tall, iron gates were open and a light burned above them. There were lights inside the yard too, spreading a glow over lorries and drays which were being loaded. Half a dozen men stood about and a gate-keeper in uniform approached when the little party entered the cobbled yard. The warehouse was spotlessly clean. Strip lighting everywhere made the huge storerooms look bright. A night-watchman took them in a lift down to the floor below, and then led them along a wide passage towards the main underground chambers. Imported and expensive goods of all kinds were stored here, he informed them.

He led them round a corner.

A man, who was standing in front of a big bin, turned and glanced at him – and at sight of Peel his expression was startled at first, then sardonic.

"Good evening, Mr Scott," Peel said gruffly. "This is Mr Jeremiah Scott, Sir Guy."

Chapter Twenty-One

Clayton's Story

Scott took out his gold cigarette-case, flipped it open and thrust it in front of Chatworth, who shook his head. Scott's grin was almost a sneer as he lit a cigarette himself.

"My, my," he said to Peel. "You get around, sergeant."

"What are doing here?" countered Peel.

"Business," said Scott. "Perriman's want a special airtight carton for some of this stuff, and I want to find out what the storage conditions are like."

"I'm not satisfied with your explanation," Peel said.

"That's all you'll get," said Jeremiah flatly.

Chatworth asked: "How long have you been here?"

"About an hour."

"How many people have you seen down here?"

"Not many – they're working upstairs tonight."

"Have you seen Inspector West?" demanded Chatworth.

Scott opened his mouth and gently rubbed the corner.

"So West's in trouble, is he? Lost him?"

Chatworth said: "Mr Scott, I don't like your manner, and I agree with Sergeant Peel that your answers have been extremely unsatisfactory. I shall ask—"

He was interrupted by a sudden exclamation from their guide, who had gone round the corner. Peel ran forward and saw their guide standing and staring at a hole in the wall. The passage was thick with rubble, bricks, and dirt. Near it were footprints and little blobs of dirt; a number of men had walked this way recently.

Peel reached the hole quickly, shone a torch inside, and stepped through.

The wall was nearly a foot thick, and beyond it was a narrow passage. The torchlight fell on crumbled earth and bricks, much the same as that at the other end of the passage. There must have been two explosions, and both ends of the tunnel were blocked.

The others joined Peel inside the hole, and Scott said softly: "Well, you've certainly found something!"

Peel switched on his torch and swivelled the beam swiftly. Next moment, the beam struck a man's foot. It travelled up the body swiftly, but before it fell upon the face, Peel knew that it wasn't Roger West.

It was Clayton.

Orders were given for digging to start at this end immediately. Clayton's head was injured, but he regained consciousness while they bent over him.

He was taken to hospital, but was unable to tell a coherent story. The escaping crooks had either left just before Scott's arrival or else he had seen them. The escape-hole was next to a small, steel door, painted the colour of the walls, and which they obviously hadn't been able to open. It had been jammed by the blast from the explosion.

Peel was in the warehouse cellar; Bill Sloan; Eddie Day, who had arrived only half an hour before, just after four o'clock – heaven knew how he had managed to learn of the trouble. There was a woman, too, from a nearby Sailors' Mission, who had brought in food and a tea urn and cups and saucers. They rattled on a hastily erected trestle-table.

And Janet was there, fetched by Chatworth, tense and pale.

The men were still working in the tunnel, and they had cleared nearly twenty feet. Janet knew that they were afraid that they might find Roger buried under the rubble.

Chatworth was talking to a big fellow to whom she had been vaguely introduced – the local superintendent. Janet watched them, rather dully. She knew now something of what the miner's wives felt like when there was a fall in the pits and their men were entombed.

Entombed …

"Oh, Mrs West." It was the Mission woman, who was just at her elbow. "I want to slip away for a few minutes to get some more bread, I wonder if you would look after the urn for me."

"The urn—oh—oh yes."

"Thank you so much."

It was good to have something to do, and the little woman probably realised it. Men, smeared with dirt, their faces streaked with perspiration, came from the tunnel and had a cup of tea and a sandwich, while others took their places; a dozen were working in relays of three, now, and there was a chain of men moving buckets of earth and pieces of rubble, dumping them in a corner of the cellar.

Someone inside the tunnel exclaimed: "Careful!"

"Found something?"

"Looks like …"

The cup fell from Janet's hand, tea splashed on to her shoes and stockings. The man waiting swung round, the tea forgotten. Chatworth and Peel sprang to Janet's side, and the little woman stopped spreading butter on the bread.

"Take it easy," a man said.

"It's his foot."

His foot!

Chatworth tightened his grip on Janet's arm but did not speak. She walked round the trestle-table towards the hole, and Chatworth went with her. She peered along the well-lighted tunnel. The lanterns were hanging at intervals of a couple of feet on each wall. She stepped through the hole, and Chatworth followed her. Now the men were standing on piles of rubble and working from the top.

She saw Roger's leg.

It was clear from the knee; one leg – no, his other leg was visible now.

Janet began to tremble.

"Easy, m'dear," said Chatworth. "Easy." He looked round. "The doctor there?"

"Waiting," said Peel. "We've got oxygen, we're all ready."

"Good."

Janet's trembling became more violent.

Chapter Twenty-Two

Clayton

CID MAN FEARED DEAD
ALL-NIGHT EFFORTS AT RESCUE

'In an underground chamber of a derelict warehouse, now known to have been used by food thieves, police and other rescue workers fight for the life of Chief Inspector Roger West of Scotland Yard. By their sides waits his anxious wife.

Earlier in the day, the Yard had tracked a gang of food racketeers to their lair. In an underground gun-battle, several men were wounded. Big stores of stolen food were found.'

***ECHO* REPORTER SAFE**
PRISONER OF FOOD GANG

'*Echo* reporter, Tommy Clayton, was rescued by the police last night after the warehouse gun-battle in the East End. In hospital, Clayton is cheerful and likely to be about again very shortly. He was captured while observing a suspect at a food factory, taken to the warehouse where he was later found, and escaped from his captors in the confusion caused by the arrival of the police.'

TRIUMPH FOR THE POLICE
HIDDEN HOARDS FOUND

'The CID quickly responded to the *Echo's* demand for urgent steps to cope with the food thieves. Within a few hours, information received led Divisional Superintendent Bellamy and Chief Inspector West of Scotland Yard to one of the main hoards – many tons of food were discovered and two arrests were made.

The *Echo* understands that none of the food discovered was that stolen from vans belonging to the Perriman company. Most of the goods were Danish or Dutch, and obviously had been smuggled ashore from ships unloading at the London Docks. The food found was …'

Roger put down the newspaper and stretched out for a cigarette. He laughed ruefully, and it was loud enough to attract Scoopy's attention.

"Is that you, Daddy?" he called from the hall.

"Yes, I'm all right, old chap."

Scoopy was already hurrying up the stairs, and in his wake came Richard and, just behind them, Marjorie Goodwin.

Janet's footsteps sounded in the hall. "Scoopy – Richard! Where are you?"

"Any chance of a cup of tea?" called Roger.

"Darling!" Janet flew up the stairs. "You're awake!"

"Hallo, my sweet."

The children watched their mother and father wide-eyed, and when Janet drew back Richard said: "Daddy's all right."

"Are you, Roger? You feel—"

"Fine!"

"Boys, you go downstairs and tell Auntie Nell that Daddy's awake," said Janet. "You go with them, Marjorie." She sat on the edge of the bed as they went off. "You *look* all right," she conceded.

"I am all right," said Roger firmly. "Bit stiff and sore in places, but nothing to worry about. How long have I been lazing in bed?"

"You've nearly slept the clock round," said Janet. "You came to in the ambulance—don't you remember us putting you to bed?—and that was just after ten o'clock yesterday morning. It's nearly half-past nine now. Oh, darling, I thought I'd lost you!"

Roger gripped her hand.

In the pause, Nell Goodwin appeared in the doorway with a tea-tray. She didn't stay long, and Janet poured out tea.

The front-door bell rang and Janet went downstairs. Roger heard a man's voice, next Janet's, rather uncertain, and then he recognised a curious little laugh. Tommy Clayton had called!

"Send him up!" called Roger.

"Please don't stay too long," said Janet. "All right," she called to Roger, and then showed Clayton up to the bedroom.

Like Roger, he had some scratches and bruises, but his eyes were clear and he looked well and cheerful. He was dressed in a pair of flannels and a black-and-white check sports jacket! Roger looked at the jacket ruefully as the reporter sat down.

"Do you buy them by the dozen?" he asked.

Clayton chuckled.

"Managed to get hold of a length of cloth, and there was enough for two coats," he said. "Just as well, the other one isn't exactly wearable. Any idea who the cove was in the dump?"

"Not yet," said Roger, "but I'm out of touch this last day or two."

"You'll soon be in it again," said Clayton dryly. "And thanks for trying to get me clear. You know that quite a lot of stuff kept in Perriman's warehouse at the docks was shifted to the other place through that passage, don't you?"

"I didn't," said Roger.

"They *are* keeping you in the dark. The hole in the Perriman warehouse wall was near a door – it was jammed and they had to break the wall down. The gang was in cahoots with a couple of Perriman's night-staff. Stuff was taken from the ships to the warehouse and lifted during the night. Stock-sheets and the rest were rigged. I'd discovered that before I went out to the Woodhall factory. There seemed to be an accomplice at Woodhall, working with the two rogues at the docks."

"How did you get on to it?" demanded Roger.

"I chanced on a story down in the docks. These two warehousemen at Perriman's slipped quite a lot of the small presents to their friends and did a little illegal trading on their own, so I followed it up and got one of them tipsy. He didn't exactly give the game away, but said enough to make me very curious about Perriman's stocks. Then you helped me a bit when you got that little chap, Relf. I knew he had a brother, and found the said brother often went to that derelict warehouse. Then he got the job at Perriman's Dispatch Department, so I hung around.

"I was too careless – they recognised me, and next time I poked my nose near the derelict warehouse after dark, they cracked me on the head. I thought it was a case of curtains. Can't quite make out why they didn't kill me. They took my clothes and left me my pants and apparel I wouldn't like to be seen dead in. They kept me in the tunnel on a bread-and-water diet."

Roger nodded.

"And they told me that they'd made arrangements to scuttle if they were discovered. Actually when you arrived, they got scared and careless. I got away, as you know. But they grabbed me, and clouted me over the head again. But something went wrong and they had to leave me behind in the tunnel. No doubt they all slipped through that hole in the wall and out of the Perriman warehouse."

"I don't know," said Roger.

"Well, Peel tells me that's what happened," said Clayton. "Now you've driven 'em out of Wignall's garage and also out of the warehouse. I wonder where they'll bob up next."

"Any ideas?"

"Not a glimmering," said Clayton. "My trail ended at Perriman's. Mind you, I think some of their staff are in the know."

"It wouldn't surprise me," said Roger.

"Run across Jeremiah Scott much?" asked Clayton, changing the subject and assuming an air of innocence.

"As the brother of Mike Scott, I've met him."

"Rum cove," said Clayton. "Seems to have the run of Perriman's. I'm told that he was at the dock warehouse when Peel and Chatworth went along there looking for you. I've checked on him quite a bit. Gets around plenty, and Perriman's aren't the only food companies he knows. More than just a salesman – he's a director of Tucktos. Doesn't just pop into the buying offices and book orders, he goes into the works, sees what the cartons and boxes are needed for, submits designs – in fact, he can pretty well go where he likes on the customers' premises."

"He's a first-class salesman," Roger remarked, "and his firm delivers the goods."

"Perhaps that's the answer. How's Mark Lessing getting on these days? Having a nice time at Brighton?" asked Clayton with a grin. "Oh yes, we know he's at the same hotel as Sybil Lennox. They're by way of being friends already, which isn't bad work on Mark's part. Trust Sybil?"

"I don't trust anyone until I prove I can," said Roger dryly.

Janet came in, to insist that Clayton had stayed long enough. Actually, the talk had stimulated rather than tired Roger, and he was eager to get to the Yard.

Instead Peel came to see him.

Peel's reports were largely negative. It was true that two men had been caught at the derelict warehouse and had talked freely. They swore that they did not know who was behind the racket. Relf and a man named Wilkins had given them their orders, but they had no idea who instructed Relf and Wilkins. On the night of the hold-ups, the warehouse had been deserted. The two prisoners confessed to taking part in an attack, but they had not known that others were taking place.

They did not know where other stores were kept.

"Find anything on them?" asked Roger, who was now up and dressed.

Peel was sitting opposite him in the front room.

"Only one thing that will interest you much," said Peel. He took an envelope from his pocket and handed it to Roger. "One from each man," he added, and Roger opened the envelope and took out two programmes; they were for the previous Fulham home match.

"Questioned them about this?" asked Roger sharply.

"No – I thought it might be wise to let it sweat."

"When are Fulham at home again?" asked Roger.

"The day after tomorrow."

Roger grinned. "We're going to see a football match! Nice to mix a bit of pleasure with duty sometimes, isn't it?"

Peel laughed.

"And there's nothing else?" said Roger.

"Well, no – you know that Randall's pal, Wilson, has been at Perriman's, don't you? He's spent a lot of time with Akerman, and he's obviously trying to make sure that he digs the Crown company well in, and keeps Tucktos out."

"Can't blame him," said Roger. "And is that the lot?"

"There have been several food robberies at shops and warehouses up and down the country. There's one queer thing too. We haven't traced a quarter of the stolen food, and I'd say that a lot of it hasn't been released. But it will be, soon, and I've been wondering how. We've always rather assumed that Perriman's themselves would be above a racket, but they've a perfect set-up for disposing of stolen stuff, haven't they? Thousands of shops."

Roger said: "I'd need a lot of convincing that they're in it. Why steal their own stuff to sell in their own shops?"

Peel leaned back.

"They get insurance for the original loss and good prices for what they sell. They could pass it on to some of their own shops too. They'd have to use the manager and possibly some of the assistants at picked shops, but it could be done. It would mean that a good flourishing business would be ruined if it were found out, which makes me wonder whether someone in Perriman's, someone high up, might be behind the racket, using the stores without the knowledge of the other directors.

"It is possible, isn't it?" insisted Peel, when Roger didn't answer.

Roger said slowly: "Yes. The seaside branches might be worth watching. We'll send word round to some of the coastal resort police and get them to keep a look out."

"I suppose Mr Lessing couldn't do anything at Brighton," murmured Peel.

"I'll have a word with him."

Peel left soon afterwards.

Mark Lessing telephoned later in the afternoon. He had nothing much to report, except that Sybil Lennox appeared to be benefiting from her rest. He saw a great deal of her, although she wasn't by any means easy to approach, and so far she wouldn't go places with him, beyond a walk along the promenade.

Roger detected the keen note in Mark's voice when he was asked to keep an eye on the Perriman branches in Brighton.

"All I want to know is, if there appears to be anything unusual – unusual type of customer, dirty work at the back door after shop hours, mysterious vans – that kind of thing. Don't *do* anything – just keep your eyes open," Roger added.

"Trust me," said Mark.

Roger was at the office next day, and had been through an accumulated mass of letters and memos when the telephone bell rang.

"Liverpool CID on the line, sir," said the operator. "Superintendent Haythorn."

"Put him through," said Roger.

A man spoke in a gruff, north-country voice.

"That Inspector West … Haythorn of Liverpool here. You may remember, we met two years back, when you came up on the Larramy job."

"Oh yes, of course – how are you?"

"I was all right," said Haythorn dryly, "but I'm not feeling so good right now. We've just discovered some big losses at the docks. Bacon and canned foods mostly, taken during the night wi'out being noticed. Must be most of a hundred tons gone, and the night-watchman with it. Reckon it's part of your business?"

"It wouldn't surprise me," said Roger heavily, and drew a pencil and paper towards him. "Fire away."

Haythorn gave him a detailed story and rang off.

Three-quarters of an hour later the telephone operator said: "Southampton CID on the line, sir."

Another port.

"Put 'em through, please."

The Southampton man's voice, oddly enough, was as broad Lancashire as Haythorn's had been; and his story was on similar lines.

Liverpool, Southampton, Plymouth, Bristol, Cardiff, Newcastle, Hull, Harwich – from all round the coast, during the next twenty-four hours, came reports of similar losses. The robberies had all been bare-faced; lorries had driven up and the stuff loaded and taken away, aided and abetted by night-watchmen or other members of the warehouse staff.

More and more reports came in from the provinces and from all over London.

Next morning the *Echo's* headlines screamed the story.

Chapter Twenty-Three

Match Winners

Just after two o'clock on the Saturday afternoon, Roger was driving away from the Yard when Chatworth drove in.

"Where are you off to?" demanded Chatworth.

"As a matter of fact, sir," said Roger, "I'm going to see Fulham play."

"You *what?* Confound it, Roger!" Chatworth was shaken. "This is hardly the time—eh? Who? Fulham?"

"Yes, sir. Peel's already there, and I've got the Divisional people watching all the turnstiles. They've got photographs of Jeremiah Scott, and several others whom we think might be concerned. Just an idea that they might make contact with one of the leaders on the ground. These programmes—"

"Well, it's one excuse for watching a football match," said Chatworth. "All right. Nothing to report?"

"Nothing, sir."

Chatworth nodded and Roger went back to his car.

It was nearly half-past two when Roger reached Stevenage Road and the Fulham ground. The queues were quite long, turnstiles were clicking, dozens of men and boys were calling: "Programmes – 'ficial programmes!" They were kept busy taking programmes out of the canvas satchels swung round their waists, making sales by the dozen. Roger walked slowly towards the stand turnstiles, and saw

Peel with a thickset man who was probably from the Fulham Police Station. Peel noticed him and raised a hand.

Roger joined him.

"Sergeant Parker, sir, of Fulham."

"Hallo, Parker," said Roger. "Nice easy job, to pick individuals out of this crowd."

"Often had to do it, sir," said Parker.

"I've fixed a seat for you in the centre stand," Peel said to Roger. "Had a word with the manager. He doesn't know what we're looking for, of course. I haven't seen Scott, but there's one man I have seen. Akerman – the Buyer at Perriman's."

"Any idea where he lives?" asked Roger thoughtfully.

"I haven't checked up, but I will. I—"

Peel hesitated, then turned his face away from Stevenage Road and looked straight at the nearest turnstiles. Roger glanced in the same direction, and Peel whispered: "Couple just getting out of the Rolls, sir – recognise them?"

"Well, well!" murmured Roger. "Samuel Perriman and the great Emanuel. Football fans!"

Neither of the Perriman directors looked round or appeared to take the slightest interest in what was going on about them.

"Let's get in," said Roger.

They went to the next entrance and presented their tickets. Beyond the entrance was the back of the stand. An iron fence kept a small part of the enclosure separate from the rest, and small boys and a few men hung about near the rails. Among these were the Perrimans.

Peel said: "Been here before, sir?"

"Not this part – I usually have my two-bob's worth," said Roger.

"Same here, sir. That's Craven Cottage." Peel pointed to a small house at a corner of the ground. "Home team's dressing-room is in there, visitors through that side door." He pointed to two cars. "Those belong to directors. The crowd's waiting for the players who pass here on their way to the field. Must be nearly ready for the kick-off."

"That's three-fifteen," said Roger.

"In ten minutes, then," said Peel. "Anyone who hasn't turned up now will have to be slippy. I can't get over that couple of Dismal Jimmies. Fancy the Perriman's—"

"Need it be a poor man's game?" came a voice behind them. They turned abruptly, to see Jeremiah Scott. The familiar half-grin, half-leer curled his lips. "Rich man, poor man, beggar-man, thief – all come to football matches. And so, obviously, do policemen. Looking for anyone?"

"We thought we might find you," said Roger dryly.

"Oh, always. Member's ticket – didn't you notice that when you went through my pockets? I like football, and so do the Perrimans." Jeremiah laughed. "Often seen them here. Akerman appears now and again, probably so that the bosses can spot him. Any other information I can give the police before I take my seat?"

"Not now, thanks," said Roger.

Jeremiah waved his programme mockingly, turned and disappeared beneath the stand.

"That man's too clever by half," growled Peel.

The enclosures were densely packed, the terraces were crowded except at the two far corners, and every barrier was crammed with people.

Roger had a seat in the third row, near the Press and only a few yards away from the Perriman brothers, who were bending over their programmes. Roger felt that someone was looking at him, turned and saw the Tucktos man's sardonic grin. Roger grinned and waved, and was at least certain that Scott hadn't expected that. Then he scanned the people near him, and saw Akerman.

A sudden roar of cheering made him glance round.

The Fulham team were coming from the corner of the ground, strapping fellows wearing white shirts and black shorts, and then the air was split with another roar, much louder than the first – Rentown taking the field.

Rentown won the toss and Fulham kicked off against a light breeze, coming from the Bishop's Park end.

It was surprising how quickly the ground emptied after the game. One minute there had been a cheering excited mass and a swarm of boys following the teams from the pitch; the next, there was quiet and the people thronged towards the exits.

Roger saw the Perriman brothers leave, followed by Akerman. Perriman's certainly supported Fulham. He lit a cigarette and a man said from his side: "Got a light, mister?"

That was Scott again.

Roger flicked his lighter.

"Thanks," said Scott. "Not a bad game, was it? Fulham just about deserved to win. See any bad men?"

"At least one," Roger said. Scott laughed.

Peel came up. "There's a drink going in the directors' room, if you feel like one, sir," he said.

"Wouldn't be a copper if he didn't," said Scott. He laughed again and turned away.

"You didn't see anything helpful, I suppose?" Peel said.

"I can't say I did," said Roger, "except the number of people in this case who've a soft spot for Fulham. I—hello, Scott's dropped something."

The tall man had dropped his programme, and Roger went and picked it up, then put it absently into his pocket.

"Any reports from our fellows?" he asked.

"Nothing at all, I'm afraid." Peel began to lead the way beneath the stand. "It would be a good place to meet, though – messages could be easily passed on, couldn't they?"

Roger nodded.

They went through a low doorway in a brick wall and found themselves in a small area – V-shaped, with one exit leading to the pitch, the other to the road. A crowd of people stood about. He saw one man nudge his companion, and recognised an *Echo* reporter. The man grinned and waved. Roger nodded and followed Peel to a side entrance to the Cottage itself. They entered a narrow passage, with doors on either side, a glass partition and a hatch, which was up, disclosing the office. The next door was open and was marked: 'Secretary's Office.'

Inside, a hundred people seemed to be talking at once. There were nine men to every woman, standing, sitting or lounging about, drinking tea, beer or whisky and eating sandwiches.

"As soon as this crowd has eased off a bit, I'll take you to see the manager," said Peel. "The more I think about those programmes found at Hurlingham, the more odd I find it, sir. Most people throw their programmes away, don't they?"

"Wouldn't say so," demurred Roger. "Not immediately after the game, anyhow."

He finished a beer, and looked up to see the *Echo* sports reporter standing in the doorway by the side of a heavily built man with a rugged, rather attractive face. The reporter was pointing at Roger, and Peel whispered: "That's Osborne, the manager."

Osborne raised a hand to attract Peel's attention and jerked his head towards the passage. Then he went out. Roger and his sergeant edged their way across the room, and found Osborne standing in the doorway of his office. Peel introduced Roger, they shook hands and Osborne said: "Come and meet our chairman of directors, Mr West. Bill"—he spoke to the steward—"shut the door and don't let anyone come in until I open it again."

The office was quite small. There was a roll-top desk in one corner, and some odd chairs, a bookshelf and some filing cabinets. Dean, the chairman of directors, was a tall, smiling man, who gave Roger the impression that he had something on his mind. But first he offered drinks.

"Enjoy the game?" he asked.

"Thoroughly," said Roger.

"The boys were at their best today," said Dean, lighting a cigarette. His hand was a little unsteady. Osborne leaned against the roll-top desk with a glass in his hand. "Yes, right on top of their form," Dean went on. "Er—Mr West …"

He broke off.

Roger smiled.

"Any particular reason for your being here today?" asked Dean. "In force, I mean – you've been watching the turnstiles and the crowd pretty closely, haven't you?"

"Never heard of pickpockets?" asked Roger lightly.

Dean said eagerly: *"Is* that why you've concentrated so much? I know the local inspector well, of course; *he* didn't say anything about a special pickpocket check today. Usually does, if one's coming off. Did you come for pickpockets?"

"Know of any other reason why we should be here?" asked Roger.

Dean and Osborne exchanged quick glances.

"As a matter of fact ..." began Dean.

"Yes, we do," said Osborne bluntly. "We may be wrong, but one of our boys is missing."

"Boys?" echoed Roger. "Do you mean players?"

"Not this time," said Osborne. He lit a cigarette, and now seemed as troubled as the chairman of directors. "This one is our assistant trainer, Maidment. Hasn't been with us long. We needed a second assistant to our trainer, and Maidment suited. Good recommendations, first-class at his job, but—"

"He's disappeared," said Dean. "Made me furiously angry when I first heard about it. Still, if he can't help it—"

"I don't quite follow you," said Roger. "How do you know whether he can help it or not?"

Osborne rubbed his long jaw, and then said: "He was here on a Tuesday afternoon last week, and that's the last we heard about him. I went to his home myself – couldn't understand why he wouldn't answer the telephone. Found the house shut up, and a policeman seemed to be watching it." Osborne grinned. "He seemed to be very interested in me until I told him who I was! And he's a fan! It's a house in Hurlingham, not very far away from here—"

"Kent Street?" interposed Roger.

Osborne said softly: "So you know something about him, Inspector?"

"I know all about that house in Kent Street," said Roger, and began to feel real excitement. "How long had he lived at the house in Kent Street?"

"He was in digs there – moved there when he got his job," said Osborne.

"Have you got his old address?" asked Roger.

"Sure, it's in the files. Like to have it?"

"Please."

"Do you know anything *against* this house in Kent Street?" asked Dean tensely.

"You might call it a home for crooks," said Roger dryly, as Osborne opened a drawer in a filing cabinet and rummaged through some papers. "What build was he?"

"Well—" began Dean.

"Bill!" called Osborne, and immediately the door opened and the steward appeared. He was rather shorter than medium height and plump. "That's about his figure," said Osborne. "You'd say you were about the same weight as Maidment, wouldn't you, Bill?"

"Not a couple of pounds different," said Bill, standing quite still, while Roger eyed him up and down and thought that he was remarkably like Tommy Clayton in build.

Bill took himself off, while Osborne handed Roger a letter. It was written in careful, rather schoolboyish handwriting, and was a formal application for the post of second assistant trainer. The address was Manor Park, E12.

"Now, Inspector, why *did* you come here? It wasn't after the dips – you needn't try that one on me. Is it about these murders?" Osborne asked bluntly.

Roger said: "It could be. As a matter of fact, we found some of your programmes at this Kent Street house, and one or two people we've pulled in have had programmes in their pockets. So we checked to see if any suspects came here today. Drew a blank, as far as I can find out," he added.

Maidment had lived at the Manor Park address for two years. He was a single man, and his landlady knew very little about him, but she did know his dentist. So, at half-past eight that night, Roger went to see the dentist, who was reluctant to leave his fireside, but agreed to come to the Yard and bring with him his records of the work done on the mouth of Mr Maidment.

By ten o'clock Roger knew that the body in the dump at Woodhall was that of the assistant trainer.

"Now we *know* that the Fulham programmes mean something," Roger said to Peel, when the dentist had gone. They were in the CI's office, with all the lights on; elsewhere the Yard seemed quiet and deserted, and Peel looked tired.

"You'd better get home. Tomorrow may be Sunday, but it won't be a day of rest for us. The reports from the Fulham ground are all here, aren't they?" said Roger.

Peel tapped a Manila folder.

"All in there."

In the quiet of the office, Roger read through the reports from the Divisional police and his own men. There was one on Samuel and Emanuel Perriman; another on Jeremiah Scott; a third on Akerman; another on the Woodhall Dispatch Department foreman, more about other employees of Perriman's, three on taxi-drivers, who usually garaged their taxis at Wignall's garage, and several more on friends or acquaintances of one or the other of the Relfs. Was it really so astonishing that so many people on the fringe of the Randall case had been to see that match? Would they have gone to see the game itself? There was no immediate answer, and on the whole it seemed to Roger that a detached critic might say that he was reading more than there was into the Fulham ground coincidence. He read each report closely; all were brief, and the one on the Woodhall foreman was typical:

'Arthur Morgan. Arrived at ground, 2:51pm on foot, with two companions from Perriman's, Woodhall. Bought programme from seller outside Bishop's Park gate adjacent to ground. Entered covered terraces through turnstile K. Took up position half-way between Cottage goal-line and centre of field. Showed great enthusiasm when Fulham goals were scored. No one else approached him. Left ground at 5:03pm and walked through Bishop's Park to Putney Bridge, where he caught a number 22 bus, going to Homerton.'

Roger flipped over the report and glanced at the next – and when he did so something which was in most of the reports struck him so forcibly that he sat back sharply in his chair. This was the report on Jeremiah Scott, who had also bought his programme from the seller whose pitch was by the park gates next to the ground.

Everyone remotely associated with the case had bought a programme from the same man!

Chapter Twenty-Four

Programme!

Roger took out Jeremiah's programme, and placed it side by side with his own. The printing on Scott's programme was slightly larger than on his, and the margins were a little smaller. The paper was different too.

Roger read one paragraph from his own programme, then the same one from Scott's. They were identical in most respects, but there were several misprints in Scott's which didn't appear in his. Odd letters, words slightly misspelt, something which might mean a code, but –they certainly hadn't been printed on the same machine.

He lit a cigarette, conscious of a rising excitement.

He finished reading *Club Chatter* in Scott's programme, and the final sentence was:

> 'We regret that next week's programme might not be so detailed. This will be corrected at the earliest opportunity.'

He read his own again – that sentence wasn't in it.

"Now we've got something," he said aloud, nicking over the pages of the directory on his desk, and looked up Osborne's home telephone number. He put the call in, and was waiting for it to come through when he heard footsteps in the passage outside. Then Chatworth came in.

"Oh, hallo, sir," said Roger brightly.

"Making up for lost time?" asked Chatworth, rather tartly.

The telephone bell rang.

"I won't be a moment, sir ... Hallo ... Is that Mr Frank Osborne?"

"Yes, who's that?"

"West here – Inspector West. Sorry to worry you again, but I'm interested in your programmes. Do you have them printed by two different people?"

"We do not," said Osborne.

Roger said: "Did you have this sentence in this week's programme? 'We regret next week's programme might not be so detailed. This will be corrected at the earliest opportunity.'"

"The man who wrote that must be daft," said Osborne. "The programme will be exactly the same next week – except that it's a London Combination game, not a League match. What put the idea into your head, Inspector?"

"I've two different programmes of today's match," said Roger slowly. "They're identical in wording, except for that sentence, but they were printed on different machines and on different paper."

"It could be a pirate programme," said Osborne. "That's happened before. Someone prints the teams and makes the thing look like an official job, and gets a rake-off."

"This has everything the official one has," said Roger.

"Then it's not simple pirating," commented Osborne. "You wouldn't know what pitch it was bought from, would you?"

"Yes. By the park gates, next to the ground."

"Was it, then?" exclaimed Osborne. "That pitch is held by a friend of Maidment. It fell vacant a few months ago, and Maidment said he knew a youngster who would like the job."

"Can you tell me where I can find him?" demanded Roger.

"Now that's just what I can't do," said Osborne. "He reports to the office before each match, and pays for the programmes he's sold afterwards. I'll make inquiries, if you like."

"Better leave that to me," said Roger.

"If that's the way you want it, all right," said Osborne. "Shall I tell you if the boy turns up at the next match?"

"Or before," said Roger. "We'll be watching for him next week. Thanks very much, Mr Osborne, good night."

He rang off, glancing at Chatworth, who said gruffly: "Well, what's it all about?"

Roger told him.

Chatworth made little comment, but agreed that the journey to Fulham looked as if it would yield dividends. Then a sergeant came in.

"Another report for you, sir – from the South-West Division," the sergeant said. "Just been brought in, sir – the man who made it met with a slight accident, that caused the delay. It's been sent by special messenger."

"Thanks," said Roger, taking the report.

The sergeant went out, and Roger slit open the envelope. His attention sharpened when he started to read.

"Now what's this?" demanded Chatworth.

"Listen to this, sir," said Roger eagerly. "'A woman answering the description of Sybil Lennox arrived at the Fulham football ground at 3:05pm in a taxi, entered the park-end terraces, paying 2/- after buying a programme from a man at the park gates. She was approached by five or six men during the afternoon, and engaged in conversation with each of them for several minutes."

Roger put the report down, and his eyes were hard and bright.

"If she came up from Brighton, why didn't we know?" Chatworth demanded. "What's Mark Lessing doing?"

"I'll go down to Brighton and find out," said Roger.

All was not well with Sybil Lennox.

There was nothing on which Mark Lessing could put his finger; nothing worth reporting to Roger. It might have been that the girl was still suffering from shock after Randall's death – and yet Mark had a feeling that it was something other than that. Sometimes she was almost gay and took part in the general conversation at the hotel; at other times she would shut herself in her room. Once or twice she received letters and telephone calls. The previous evening they had gone to the theatre together, and Mark had found that it mattered whether she wanted his company or not.

It would not be easy to behave dispassionately over a girl of whom he was getting fond. If Roger suspected, he would send someone down from the Yard to watch her. Mark had, in fact, debated with himself as to the wisdom and fairness of telling Roger about it, but had decided to leave it until after the weekend.

Brighton FC were playing at home.

After the theatre, Mark had suggested that she might care to watch a football match, and she had agreed. Next morning – that Saturday morning – just after eleven o'clock, when he had been sitting in the writing-room, she had come in, and said abruptly: "Mr Lessing, I'm sorry, I won't be able to come this afternoon."

"Oh?" He felt ludicrous because he showed his disappointment so clearly.

"I'm sorry, but I have to meet some friends," she said, and went out.

Mark had been a little way behind the girl when she had left the hotel and had walked rapidly towards the main shopping centre. He'd followed as far as the Dome, and then she had disappeared into a shop. He wasn't sure which one, but he knew that it was one of several near a large cinema. So he had strolled as far as the three shops and looked into each.

Sybil hadn't been in any of them. One was a Perriman branch.

He had gone across the road, and stood looking in a shop window for some time and had seen a taxi draw up outside the shop. He had been able to see the girl's reflection in the shop window as she hurried out of Perriman's and stepped into the cab. By a lucky chance, another taxi near by was empty. Mark had followed the first to the railway station, and saw Sybil go on to the platform for the London trains.

She travelled first.

He travelled third.

Just after three o'clock she had reached the Fulham ground.

He had taken up a position some way behind her, and had not been able to see so much as the detective whose report Roger received later. He had seen several men speak to her after forcing their way through the crowd.

Being afraid of losing her on the way out, Mark had left a few minutes before the final whistle, and had been waiting at the exit. He had caught sight of her broad-brimmed hat as it bobbed up and down among the people. She had joined the queue waiting for trolley-buses, and then gone to Hammersmith, from Hammersmith to Victoria and then to the Brighton platform.

Now they were back at the hotel – it was a little past eight.

He doubted whether she knew he had followed her all day.

She looked up as he entered the lounge after dinner, and her smile seemed to invite him to sit in the chair next to her.

"It's almost a pity we went to the theatre last night, isn't it?" he said.

"What makes you say that?"

"Well, if we hadn't gone we could go tonight."

She laughed. "Oh, I see."

"We could try the flicks," suggested Mark. "Care to?"

"I don't think I'd like to go to the pictures, thank you, but ..." She paused.

"A walk?" suggested Mark quickly.

"It would be pleasant, it's a lovely night."

"Perfect," said Mark.

They dawdled over coffee, and then Sybil went upstairs for her coat. She was soon down. Her head was bare, she wore a three-quarter length beaver coat and carried a small handbag and a pair of gloves.

"Sea-front or the back streets?" asked Mark.

She laughed again – and he thought that he detected a nervous note in the sound.

"I know it's rather silly," she said, "but I'd rather like to go on the pier."

"What's silly about that?" demanded Mark. "Let's go."

The main promenade was fairly well lighted, although it was gloomy in places. Couples walked arm-in-arm, murmuring to each other; a little party of girls in their early teens came walking along slowly, giggling among themselves. Two youths stood in the darkest spot, staring – at the girls or at Sybil – Mark had no idea which.

From across the road there had appeared to be a few people near the promenade, but now there proved to be hundreds. A man who had been sitting in the shadows stood up suddenly; Sybil caught her breath and clutched Mark's arm. He didn't laugh at her or speak reassuringly; his own heart was beating uncomfortably fast.

The pier loomed nearer, not brightly lighted yet. Mark and Sybil walked more slowly. If she would talk about it, she might feel better and he more courageous.

He said: "Sybil, what *is* worrying you?"

He hadn't used her Christian name before.

"Nothing!" she declared, almost too loudly.

Two youths approached close to them, swaggering along and looking as if they were determined to force Mark and the girl to get out of their way. The two youths parted, one going one side, one the other, when they were only a few yards away. Then a car drew up to the kerb, a powerful car. Mark glanced at it involuntarily – and then one of the men reached his side, pressed something into his ribs and spoke very softly: "Don't make a fuss. Get in."

"What the devil—"

The man stood grinning at Mark, pressing the 'Something' into his ribs.

"In," the man repeated.

Now Sybil was clutching Mark's arm. Mark knew that the other fellow was talking to her, in a sibilant undertone. The pressure in his ribs increased.

"*In,*" the man said again, and now menace was added to his voice as well as the thing in Mark's ribs.

Chapter Twenty-Five

Going Places

It wasn't only pressing now; it caused a sharp pain, as if the point of the knife were piercing Mark's flesh. He could just see the man's face, the half-smile that was really a sneer. To passers-by this must look like a chance encounter, a meeting of friends. The engine of the car was ticking over softly, a man in a peaked cap sat at the wheel. There were fifty people within as many yards of the car. Mark stood quite still with the sharp pain in his side, Sybil close to him. Her grip on his forearm was vice-like. Mark's assailant said: "Now listen, Lessing, I'm not going to wait all night. I'll slash the dame's face if you don't get in."

He moved his knife, swiftly, pressed it sharply into Mark's belly.

Mark jabbed at his chin – and won by surprise. The man reeled back, something dropped to the pavement with a metallic sound – the knife. The man on Sybil's other side took her arm and twisted viciously, making her gasp and release her hold on Mark's arm. She was dragged away. Mark tried to stop her, but the man he had hit now kicked at his groin. The blow landed painfully on the inside of the thigh. Sybil was now near the open door of the car. A group of girls near by stared in astonished silence.

Mark shouted: *"Police!"*

A figure loomed close to him, a hand moved near his face, and he saw a light glinting on steel. He backed away. *"Police!"*

A girl screamed.

Sybil was now half-way inside the car.

Mark's second assailant blocked his path when he tried to reach her. His first had fully recovered from the attack and kicked again, getting Mark in the pit of the stomach and forcing him to stagger back, drawing in an agonised breath. Lights went in wild circles, he could no longer see steel, or faces, or the car; he could only cry out at the top of his voice: *"Help! Help!"*

And there came the sound of footsteps of men running.

The blurred and circling lights steadied, but before he could see clearly or tell whether help was at hand, his legs were swept from under him arid he fell heavily. He heard a door slam and the car moved off.

Two youths were running towards Mark, as well as a girl. Not far away, a whistle sounded – so the police had heard the cry.

A man bent over Mark.

"You okay?"

Mark gasped: "Car—got my girl—car!"

"They're after it," the man said laconically.

Then a policeman came up …

The policeman was efficient and reassuring. The cry for help had soon been heard, one of his colleagues had commandeered a car and was giving chase. Meanwhile, as soon as the gentleman was better he would like some information. His girl had been kidnapped, according to one of the youths – was that the truth? Who was she, where had she come from, what was she dressed in?

Mark said: "Listen, constable. Telephone Scotland Yard, with a message for Chief Inspector West. Tell him that Miss Lennox—got that?—Miss *Lennox* has been kidnapped."

"Scotland *Yard*, sir?"

"Yes."

A police-car drew up.

"Better come with me to the station, sir," said the constable, "we can get through quicker from there."

It was a sleek, powerful car, and it threw off the challenge of a commandeered Morris disdainfully, lost itself in the warren of back streets in Brighton, threaded its way softly and stealthily towards the London road, hummed along for a few miles, swung off the main road into a narrow lane, and came to a standstill.

The man sitting next to Sybil said: "Out."

She fumbled for the handle of the door, just visible in the reflected light from the headlamps, and managed to open the door and stagger out of the car. She missed her footing, for the car was close to the hedge and there was a shallow ditch. Her right foot went ankle deep in water, and the cold chilled her through.

Mark's assailant, who had been sitting next to the driver, had also climbed out. He took her arm and hauled her out of the ditch. The man who had ordered her to get out now followed. He said something to the driver, who let in the clutch. The engine hummed again, tyres crunched on gravel, and then the car moved furtively off, using only the sidelights. Some distance behind them, cars travelling along the main road cast great beams, but the lights did not spread as far as this spot.

A man gripped Sybil on either side, holding her just above the elbows.

"Come on," one of them said.

They were dark, shadowy figures; their faces were just pale blurs, grotesque, frightening. Sybil was panting, as if she had been running a long way, and her legs were so weak that she knew she would fall if it weren't for the support of the two men. They went on for a hundred yards or so along the by-road in the wake of the car which had completely disappeared, and then one of the men said: "This is it."

Something white loomed out of the gloom on their left – a gate. She saw, when she was closer, that it was a five-barred gate to a field, not to the drive of a house. It groaned as it was pushed open. They went through the gate on to rough meadow-land.

Above, the stars were bright and clear, and there was no wind. Some way off, Sybil could see a myriad of lights, a great patch of darkness and then jutting arms of light, and she knew she was on high ground, overlooking Brighton – the jutting arms were the piers.

On they went.

Something came between them and the lights and the dark Channel. Trees, or a hill, or even a house cut the view off. There was now no light at all, but the men seemed to know the spot well and they didn't slacken their pace. She was half-dragged along, her ankles kept turning over – and then she trod on a hump and her shoe came off.

She resisted their pressure.

"I've lost my shoe!"

"Never mind your—"

"My shoe!"

They wouldn't stop and go back for it, so she hobbled along, her stockinged foot on the grass which felt very cold. The other shoe came off when they had gone another hundred yards or so, and she was able to walk more evenly.

As soon as they had passed through a gate, she trod on gravel. Sharp, pointed pieces cut her feet; it was agony to walk and yet she wasn't allowed to slow down. Soon she saw another open gate, and was dragged through it towards a building – house or barn, she couldn't be sure which. A torch flashed and showed a car inside an open shed.

The man with the torch called out: "Where's Lessing?"

"He ducked."

The man waiting near the car said: *"He* won't like that."

"I don't give a damn what he'll like," said her captor. "We didn't do so badly to get her." At last they released her.

It was agony to stand, but there was nowhere to sit except on the running-board of the car, and the way to that was blocked.

"She talked?" the waiting man asked. "I don't think she'll give much trouble. Take her over to a box and let her sit down. We'll be back."

Only one man was left with Sybil.

Once she was sitting on an upturned box, the relief was exquisite. There was something rather hard but not painful beneath her feet;

it rustled a little, and she realised that it was hay or straw. The torch went out. How long she stayed there, she had no idea. An hour? More? She was both dazed and frightened. Now and again she heard a man move, and knew she was being watched all the time. Then the others came back. One of the men was doing something which took him some time. The others lit cigarettes. Soon a lamp gave a mellow flame; it was a hurricane lamp, and the man who had lit it hung it on a long nail which jutted out from the whitewashed wall. The lamp spread a cosy glow about the corner of the barn, showing the bonnet of the car, a pile of straw, a square block of tightly compressed hay, and some farm implements including a scythe with the blade wrapped in hessian.

The three men stood in front of her, in a half circle.

The spokesman stood in the middle. He was the tallest of the three, and his eyes glinted. His face was blacked now, so that he could not be recognised. He drew on his cigarette and made the tip glow, then suddenly he shot out his hand, buried his fingers in her hair, and thrust her head back. At the same time, he brought the edge of his other hand down sharply on her taut throat. The blow made her gulp, the air seemed to be drawn out of her lungs, she couldn't breathe. It was all over in a moment, and when she was able to see again, he was standing in the middle of the trio, as if he had not moved.

He said: "Listen, Sybil, I'm going to ask a lot of questions, and you're going to answer every one of them. If you don't, then ..." He shrugged his shoulders. "We could do a lot of things to you, things you wouldn't care to remember."

She nodded.

"Why did you go around with Lessing?"

"He ... was friendly."

"So he was friendly," sneered her questioner. "You knew he was a pal of West's. Why—"

"I didn't!" she burst out. "It isn't true!"

"Mark Lessing is an old buddy of the great Roger West," said the man. "You're saying that you didn't know?"

"Of course I didn't!"

"I'm not so sure I believe you," said the man, and he moved his hand forward slowly. She shrank away. He didn't touch her this time, but went on: "Did you know Lessing followed you to Fulham this afternoon?"

"No!"

"Well, he did," said the man. "So you went to Fulham and made the contacts we told you to make, and Lessing watched you. That ground was lousy with policemen this afternoon, it's a cinch that you were seen. Even if you weren't, Lessing will have told his buddy by now where you went. That means they're on to us at Fulham. That's *very* bad, Sybil. Did you tell them in the first place that we sometimes met on the ground?"

"No!"

"Oh no," sneered the man. "Now, think about what you've said to Lessing. You knew who he was all right. He was down here to make you talk because West didn't believe you'd told everything. West thought that a smooth guy like Lessing could get the rest out of you. How much did you tell him?"

"Nothing! I didn't know who he was!"

The man glanced first at one companion and then at another. In that interval, Sybil's fear grew into terror – it was as if she could read the thoughts in their minds, the things they were prepared to do to make her tell the 'truth.' Then the man stretched forward, pulled open her coat, thrust it back so that her arms were forced behind her and her chest was thrust forward. One of the others slipped behind her, and fiddled with the coat; he fastened it in some way, so that her arms were pinioned and she couldn't move them. She sat precariously on the box, staring at her captors.

"How much did you tell Lessing?" the man asked.

"Nothing!"

"Now, be sensible, Sybil," the man said. "We don't want to hurt you for the sake of it, but we've got to have the truth, and we're going to get it."

One of the others stepped to the wall, and she saw him touch the handle of the wrapped scythe. He bent down, and she couldn't tear her eyes away from him. He took out a small knife which glittered, and then he cut the hessian, ripping it so that the bare, cruel blade of the scythe showed.

The spokesman stepped forward again and touched her neck – then laid his forearm across her, his hand touching one shoulder, his elbow near the other. He moved his arm sideways in a quick slicing movement, and said: "Now, if that was the scythe instead of my arm, a lot of what you've got now wouldn't be there, Sybil. Afterwards you wouldn't be such a catch. How much did you tell Lessing?"

"I didn't tell him a thing."

The man said: "He went to see the store – Perriman's. He hung about there a lot. Why?"

"I don't know! I didn't know he did!"

His arm was pressing against her again, and the man with the scythe made sweeping motions through the air, sideways and downwards – as if he were practising.

"You told him that he might learn plenty from that shop," the man insisted in his harsh, hateful voice.

"It's not true!"

Silence again.

One of the others said slowly: "She won't talk until she feels what that blade's like. Better—"

The other man raised the scythe.

Sybil stared at it, her eyes rounded pools of dread – and then she screamed. The man leapt forward again and pressed his hand tightly over her mouth, one finger poking her in the eye. She bit at his palm, but her teeth slid over it. He put his other hand to her hair and gripped and began to twist.

He let her go, and spoke in a quiet, evil voice. "Now you know what to expect, Sybil, and we'll give you just one more chance to tell us what you told Lessing."

She gasped: "I didn't—tell him—anything!"

The man said sharply: "Okay, let her have it."

She opened her mouth to scream again, but before she uttered a sound, he thrust a screwed-up handkerchief between her teeth. It made her choke and gasp. She wriggled, but her arms were still locked by the coat and there was nothing she could do. Out of the corner of her eyes she saw the glittering scythe.

And then a powerful light shone out, illuminating the scythe, and three men, and Sybil. The men swung round in startled silence. A shot rang out. The scythe clattered to the ground.

The men began to run.

They didn't get far.

A cordon of police had been flung round the barn, and among them were Roger and Mark Lessing.

Sybil was sitting in an easy chair in the hotel. Her feet had been bathed; they would be sore for a few days, but there was nothing much the matter with them or with her.

Mark sat astride an upright chair near her, leaning on the back and looking at her intently. Roger stood by the fireplace in the big bedroom. By the girl's side were coffee and sandwiches, the men had beer in tankards.

It was about two hours since they had returned from the barn. Roger hadn't pressed Sybil with questions, but had let Mark tell her what had happened after the kidnapping.

It was simple enough. Radio calls for immediate help had been sent, and had reached the Brighton Police-Station just as Roger had arrived – Mark, of course, had learned there that the CI was on his way to Brighton. The car in which Sybil had been taken away had been seen near the narrow turning by a patrol car. Police had followed the three men and Sybil.

They had heard the questions and Sybil's answers. There was something surprising in Roger West's informality. So far, Roger hadn't asked a single question. And now Mark began to speak.

"Look here, Sybil, you know enough about these beggars now to be sure they'll give you a hell of a time if they catch you again – and that whatever they're doing has to be stopped. They killed Guy Randall. They killed Relf, Kirby, and others – and there's no telling where they'll stop if they're allowed to go on. They scared you into keeping something back from Roger – you've got to tell us everything now."

Sybil moistened her lips.

"We all know you're scared, and that's why you didn't tell the whole truth," Mark went on. "But this time – well, if you won't come across, Roger won't have any alternative, you'll have to be charged with conspiracy."

She didn't comment.

"Make a start with this," Roger advised. "Why did you keep something back from us after you'd told us so much? Was it just that you were frightened of what they would do to you if you talked?"

"Yes," said Sybil at last. "I thought—they might—let me alone if I didn't tell you everything."

Chapter Twenty-Six

Main Road

Sybil Lennox told the rest of her story between one and two o'clock.

Then Roger left her at the hotel, with a cordon of Brighton police surrounding it, and went with Peel to his car and headed for London.

The wounded prisoner, the most important of the three, was in hospital with a damaged thigh-bone; so far he had refused to talk. The other two had been taken ahead, to London, and would be at Cannon Row long before Roger.

While at the wheel, Roger thought a lot about the girl's story. He had been disposed to believe her at first, now he was extremely doubtful. She had known that the Fulham ground was used by the gang, and that some of Perriman's shops were also used. She said she only knew of the Brighton one, and she didn't know to what use it was put. Nor did she know whether the ground at Craven Cottage was used for anything else than a meeting-place during matches.

For the first day at Brighton she had been unmolested. Afterwards she had received a telephone call and been told to call at Perriman's branch, where she had seen the manager, a man named Kortright. He had simply told her she was still under observation by 'them,' and warned her not to tell the police more than she had already told them.

On the Saturday morning Kortright had called her again and told her to go to Fulham and give notes – sealed notes – to men who would accost her and show her a programme with the corners all torn off; she had done so.

Kortright lived over the shop, which the Brighton police were watching. Roger had decided not to raid the shop yet.

Mark was staying at the hotel; Roger had a good idea how the land lay there. His friend was unimportant, but why *had* they used the girl again?

They realised he was on the track of the football ground and the Brighton Perriman's. They might have sent her to the match and let her give the notes to men with torn programmes, knowing that sooner or later she would tell him about that and – he reasoned – convince him that the secret of the Craven Cottage programmes was in the torn corners. But why the kidnapping? And why had her tormentor kept asking exactly what she had told Mark or the police?

Roger's thoughts faded when a lorry approached and passed, without dipping its headlights.

Peel sat by his side, dozing.

Here and there a car passed them, coming from the opposite direction; nothing overtook them. There was a thrill to be got out of speed.

There was a set smile on his lips as his foot pressed down – eighty-nine – eighty-nine point five – ninety!

Then he glanced up, and saw in the driving-mirror the headlights of the other car behind him.

They gave him a shock, because he hadn't passed anything for the last quarter of an hour. This car must have turned out of a side-road, and would soon fall behind. The needle was down to eighty-five now.

He was still travelling at more than eighty miles an hour, and yet the other car *was* gaining.

He glanced at Peel, who was snoring slightly, and then into the driving-mirror again. No doubt about it, he was being overtaken – and with some ease. Powerful bus, undoubtedly – interesting to see what it was when it passed.

Whoooooosh!

It was past.

Involuntarily, he had slowed down to the middle seventies, but the other car had left him standing; it must be doing nearly a hundred. He hadn't had time to be certain what it was, but the glimpse had made him guess at a Rolls-Royce.

The Perriman brothers had arrived at Fulham in a Rolls-Royce, but he couldn't imagine Mr Emanuel or, for that matter, the dyspeptic Mr Samuel, driving a car at nearly a hundred miles an hour on any road or in any circumstances.

The Rolls was well ahead now, but not so far as he might have expected – it had slowed down a little. The number-plate was obscured. Roger frowned. A car was coming in the opposite direction, and its headlamps created a blaze of light. Then the Rolls driver dipped his, so did the approaching car. Roger followed suit, and for a few seconds he couldn't see far ahead.

Peel grunted and stirred.

The Rolls-Royce was out of sight, round a corner; he probably wouldn't see it again.

Slower round the corner.

"I've been asleep," muttered Peel.

"Not really," said Roger sarcastically.

"Just dropped off," said Peel apologetically, and yawned. "Not so fresh as I was. I think I need a break, sir."

"Put in for one when this show is over," said Roger, turning the corner. "I—"

"*Look out!*" gasped Peel in a screech.

Roger needed no telling.

A man lay in the road ahead of him, an inert figure, lying on his face. He'd been knocked down, that Rolls-Royce – damn the Rolls! There was a little space, which should be just sufficient for Roger to squeeze through without touching the man. Was this a trick? He had just time to glance right and left, to massed trees which grew close to the side of the road. Men could be hiding in there. If he slowed down, it was possible that he would be attacked or fired at.

The man in the road hadn't moved, and now Roger could see that there was a pool of blood near his head. Roger swung across to the near-side and felt the wheels bumping over the grass verge as he passed the victim. That red splotch wasn't imagination, and meant only one thing – the man had been run down; there was nothing faked about this. He must stop, although – he couldn't help wondering ... Still, he had no choice. He pulled up on the verge, and found himself sweating freely.

Peel had already opened the car door, but Roger called out: "Wait a minute."

"Why?"

"Not too happy about the situation," Roger said quietly, and looked at the dark mass of brooding trees.

"That's no decoy!" Peel declared.

They got out, and went to the body. There was no doubt at all that the man was dead.

"Here's another car," said Roger sharply.

It was some way off, just a blaze of headlights coming from Brighton. The light lent more mystery to the night and more horror to that still figure and the scarlet splash. It grew brighter as the car approached. By now the driver must have seen the body. He swerved to one side and flashed past. The driver didn't glance at them. They caught a glimpse of him, from their own headlights. As soon as he had passed, Peel said sharply: "See him?"

"Yes, I saw him," said Roger slowly. "You wouldn't expect Tommy Clayton to worry about a roadside corpse if he were on a job, would you?" asked Roger, and he gave an odd little laugh. "I didn't think Clayton would be on the job again so quickly, did you?"

"He ought to be—"

"Never mind what ought to happen to him," said Roger. "I suppose it *was* Clayton."

"You couldn't mistake him," said Peel. "I wouldn't mind betting that the *Echo* has the whole story of the girl's kidnapping in the morning. Do you know, sir, I've never—"

Peel broke off and coughed.

"Go on," said Roger.

"I've never liked Clayton," said Peel, rather defiantly. "I wondered almost from the beginning whether that attack on him at the warehouse was faked. After all—" He broke off again and laughed rather uncertainly. "Afraid I'm letting my imagination run riot, and we should have a look at the corpse."

"Never mind, imagine some more."

"Well – Clayton could easily have told us how much he knew. We should have been at the job a lot earlier if he'd done that. And then there's the way he was kidnapped – not very convincing, when you think of it, was it?" Peel waited for no answer, but went on: "And when he escaped, or appeared to, in that warehouse, it struck me that they didn't try very hard to kill him, or they'd have succeeded. When we picked him up, he wasn't badly hurt. We've never had a really satisfactory explanation of why he was left alive, have we? That's one of the mysteries which we haven't been able to answer. And why did they dress the man Maidment up in his clothes, to make it look as if Clayton were dead. If you ask me, Clayton was going to disappear and turn up again under another name, but something went wrong, he was needed as Clayton, so they 'let' him go. What I'm really saying is," Peel went on, again defiantly, "that Clayton might be one of *them,* sir. But if I told anyone else that I thought he was, I'd be laughed out of court."

Roger said: "We won't take it to court yet, old chap. Now let's have a closer look at the corpse."

The dead man was quite young; in his early twenties. His head was badly injured, but his face hardly touched. They needed only a few minutes examination to know that he hadn't been knocked down by a car, but thrown out of one, on his head.

Peel said in a quiet voice: "I've a feeling I've seen him before, sir."

"So have I," said Roger. "I can't place him, though."

"I can't help thinking it's something to do with Saturday," said Peel.

Roger exclaimed: "I've placed him! It's that—"

"Programme seller!" cried Peel,

They stared down at the pale, lifeless face; and they could picture the youth, standing near the Bishop's Park gate, calling *'programme, 'ficial programme'* and dishing out the programmes for the twopences, the click of the coins in his little bag, and the bulging sides of his canvas satchel. It was undoubtedly the man they had wanted to question – another link in the chain had broken.

"Now, we must find a telephone," said Roger quietly. "You take the car and drive on a bit."

Peel did not have far to go. Roger was bending over the dead youth when he heard Peel shout and, looking round, saw the sergeant getting out of the car and waving to him. Roger hurried up, to find Peel standing on the grass and pointing to something which stood just inside a field gate. It was a London taxi.

They went near, flashing their torches.

The body was painted dark-blue, the chassis black, and the nearside front wing was patched. This was Kirby's taxi.

"I'll bet the kid drove it down here, and met his murderers by appointment," said Peel gruffly.

They were near Redhill, and the local police were soon on the spot.

Roger took everything that was found in the lad's pockets, left instructions that the body be sent to London, and then drove on, much more slowly than on the early part of the journey.

At Cannon Row, he spent half an hour interrogating the two prisoners there; both said that they received their orders from the third man, whose name was Smith. Roger had already charged them with attempting to cause grievous bodily harm to Sybil Lennox.

He gave instructions for them to be questioned every hour until he came again, and then went to his office. The first thing he did was to have a check made on the movements of the Perrimans' Rolls-Royce.

Nothing of interest had come in.

He sent Peel home, glanced through the contents of the dead lad's pockets again, finding two Fulham programmes. The murder, the inhuman treatment planned for Sybil Lennox, all these and other things indicated the ruthlessness of the men he was fighting. The food thefts might only be the forerunners of many others.

He reached Chelsea a little after six o'clock.

And he found himself thinking a great deal about Tommy Clayton.

Janet stirred and woke. He wouldn't let her get up, but undressed quickly and slipped into bed.

When he woke up, the sun was high and he thought that it must be approaching midday. He stretched out his hand for his watch. Half-past ten – that wasn't really too bad, he could be at the office by half-past eleven.

Janet came in.

"Ever hear of a policeman who was sacked for being late at the office?" demanded Roger.

"If there's one thing I'd love to hear, it's that you'd been given the sack," retorted Janet. "Tea? The kettle's on, I usually have a cup about this time of morning."

"None for Nell Goodwin?"

"She's gone," said Janet, and laughed at his surprise. "She said she couldn't stay on indefinitely. Jack's out of danger now, and there was a lot that wanted doing at the flat; so she left just after breakfast." She tossed him a morning paper. He yawned and stretched, felt as if he could conquer the world, and picked up the newspaper.

It was the *Echo*.

And the headline which screamed along the front page was:

GIRL TORTURED IN BARN
POLICE POUNCE

Immediately beneath it was a large photograph, head and shoulders only, of Sybil Lennox. There followed a story, reasonably accurate in detail, quite sufficient to convince him that Tommy Clayton had been near the barn the previous night; even the scythe was mentioned.

Chapter Twenty-Seven

Says Jeremiah

A frowning Chatworth sat behind his big black-topped desk. Roger sat in front of him. Chatworth was heavy-handed, in no mood to hear that Roger had really used the girl as a decoy.

"And this story of hers – what does it really amount to? It confirms the football ground business. Well, we hardly needed that confirmed. Also, the use of Perriman's Brighton shop – although from the report I see that you have no evidence that the shop is used by these men, only the girl's statement that it is so."

"The girl's, and the men who interrogated her," corrected Roger mildly. "We heard them."

"H'mm. Don't see that it makes much difference. And this—" Chatworth tapped a copy of the *Echo* with his forefinger. "Clayton was obviously watching her and knew exactly what happened. The way he's written up the story doesn't help. Most censorious article I've read for some time – says that we were almost criminally negligent about the girl. Even mentions Lessing as your friend. I don't like it, Roger. It was sheer chance that you learned that Sybil Lennox had been to Fulham. Your fine friend didn't take the trouble to telephone you and advise you she was leaving Brighton."

Roger said quietly: "He hadn't time, sir. And the Brighton police knew about it."

"Blaming others—"

Roger interrupted: "I'm blaming no one."

He was surprised both at the tartness of his voice and his temerity. He saw Chatworth start – and then his heart began to beat uncomfortably fast, in case he had gone too far.

"So you don't think anyone's to blame," growled Chatworth.

"No, I don't. It's been a case of trial and error, but we've recovered from our mistakes quickly and have forced the other side into a lot of mistakes themselves. You don't think they wanted to kill Kirby, Relf, Maidment, this programme seller, or anyone else, do you?" He knew that he sounded aggressive, but couldn't help himself. "We drove them hard and they killed in self-defence, just to keep us at bay. Well, they haven't succeeded. We're on to the Fulham ground, on to Perriman's shops, on to those programmes. Mike Scott is awaiting trial, and we've several others also under remand. We can be pretty sure that someone high up in Perriman's has a hand in the business, and there's someone else – such as Jeremiah Scott – who has a kind of roving commission."

Roger paused and lit a cigarette. His face was white, his voice rather clipped, and his mouth was dry; he wished at once that he hadn't lit the cigarette.

Chatworth looked at him beneath his shaggy eyebrows, his face expressionless.

"And that isn't all by a long way," Roger went on. "Before this started we'd no idea that there was so much food stolen – few reports reached the Yard. Now we know that it's a countrywide organisation. We've forced the thieves out of one hide-out and storage dump in London; we've stopped them from getting stuff straight from the ships which unload in the London Docks. We can see the whole set-up now."

He looked at the cigarette, then back at Chatworth, who didn't improve the situation by sitting and staring.

Chatworth relaxed, sitting back in his arm-chair.

"I see," he said mildly. "Most impressive. I congratulate you." He bent down and opened a cupboard in the desk; something clinked, and Roger's edginess eased immediately – he'd pulled it off! A whisky bottle and glasses appeared on the desk and Chatworth added a syphon. As he opened the bottle, he went on: "The impressive analysis wanted a finishing touch or two, I think. You let Sybil Lennox go to Brighton, unescorted except by your friend Lessing, because you thought she might be a good decoy. Why didn't you tell me?"

"If it wasn't self-evident, I thought it might as well just tick over," said Roger.

"I see. Much better to take me fully into your confidence. Must be able to rely on *you* – always have, always want to. What's the position, Roger? Do you think you can see what's really at the back of this business?"

Roger leaned forward and said very slowly: "I think this goes much farther than we yet realise. We've discovered the Fulham ground's place in the general scheme, but – why only Fulham? Why not Chelsea, The Arsenal, White Hart Lane – all of them are larger grounds. And why confine it to London? Why not spread it to the Midlands, the North, Scotland? What's to prevent these beggars from using a dozen different grounds, playing the same trick with the programmes, having their workers collect orders at the grounds?"

"Well, well," exclaimed Chatworth. "That big?"

"It could be. And Perriman's have their wholesale warehouses up and down the country – these, and the big retail shops which supply hotels and boarding-houses, could absorb all the stolen food. We've hardly begun, sir."

He had never seen Chatworth more perturbed.

"Take every man you need and get cracking," the AC ordered. "We want this thing smashed in a hurry."

Roger and Peel put all they'd got into the job, but it showed no sign of breaking. Scott remained a possible key, and when Mark Lessing telephoned to say that he was in London with Sybil, Roger said: "Mark, I want her help. Now, listen."

He talked for several minutes, rang off, and then telephoned to ask Scott to come and see him.

Later in the day, Peel took a telephone call, and said: "It's Jeremiah Scott."

"Fine," said Roger. "Have him sent up."

"Send him up, escorted," said Peel into the telephone. He replaced the receiver, pulled a shorthand notebook close, and sharpened a pencil.

Jeremiah came in, escorted to the door by a constable. Roger stood up and pointed to a chair. Peel pulled his notebook towards him.

Out came Jeremiah's slim, gold cigarette-case.

"Not now, thanks," said Roger. "I've smoked too much today – but you carry on."

"Good for the nerves, this Virginian tobacco," said Jeremiah. "Sorry you've been living on yours. Or is it, like me, just a matter of habit?"

"I always smoke a lot when I'm near the end of a case."

Jeremiah's eyebrows shot up.

"Really? Congratulations." He grinned. "Well, what can I do for you? Second thoughts after the Fulham match, or more inquiries into the mystery of the missing warehouseman?"

"Neither," said Roger. "I'm going rather farther back, to Randall and before Randall's death."

"Oh, your double," said Jeremiah. "I've often thought it was a pity you didn't hush up the fact that he was dead. You could have impersonated him pretty well, you know, and then the whole thing would have been easily solved. Sorry – I can't get out of the habit of facetiousness. I didn't know Randall very well – better have another cut at his lady love, who appears to have been in trouble again. I warned you from the beginning not to trust the lady and to look for her other friends, didn't I? Said friends have now apparently tried to scare the wits out of her – ever wondered why?"

"I know why. What made you warn me against her?"

"Not against her – her *friends*."

"Did you know much about these friends?"

"I knew enough not to like 'em."

"Why?"

"Because they were friends of my brother and weren't doing him any good. When are you going to bring that case on, by the way? It's a bit hard to hold a man indefinitely, and—"

"The longer he waits for his trial, the longer he'll live," said Roger sharply.

That got past Jeremiah's guard.

"Going a bit far, aren't you?" he demanded. "I didn't know you were going to charge him with murder. And I thought there was an unwritten law in this country about innocence being assumed."

Roger said: "My job is to find murderers."

"My brother isn't a murderer."

"I think he is. I know his friends are."

Jeremiah sat back in his chair, and lit another cigarette from the stub of his first,

"If you want to know more about my brother, it's simple. Always a wild youth. Got mixed up with more wild folks in the RAF. They trained him for wildness – ever thought of that? Didn't care a damn provided he was keyed up to kill and to whoop for joy after doing it. Bad thing, on impressionable minds. Then he went one worse, and became fond of Sybil. I don't know what that Jezebel has told you, but doubtless she's made herself out to be the wronged innocent, and last night's performance may encourage you to believe her. Don't. She is a liar born and bred. Her one object in life is to get her own way, and that way is chiefly directed towards getting money and clothes and luxury living. Facts, West."

Roger made no comment.

"Because he was infatuated, Mike allowed himself to be used by these precious friends of hers. As I've said, he was already wild. But there's no viciousness in him, and as an elder brother, I tell you I'm going to see that he gets justice. I've already arranged for counsel."

"Very interesting," said Roger perfunctorily. "Why did you really lose Perriman's business?"

Roger saw the sudden drop in Jeremiah's expression, not bewilderment, but surprise and perhaps alarm – and then the familiar smile which was just a mask to hide his true feelings.

"Surely I told you. Sam's T.T. I'm a Johnny Walker fan. The two don't mix."

"They mixed for a long time."

"Sam didn't find me out very easily. He hasn't found Wilson out, either – Randall's boss. Heavy drinker."

"Stick to the point," said Roger. "Samuel Perriman's an astute business-man. He knew about your drinking and it didn't matter to him. There was some other trouble."

"None, I assure you," said Jeremiah. "It may have been that on the night of the staff dance I flaunted my vice more than usual."

Roger said: "I've never known a man lie to the police and get away with it for long. Why did you drop your programme at Fulham on Saturday?"

Again that swift look of surprise.

"Getting clever now, are you?" murmured Jeremiah. "I like to think I'm getting value from the old taxes. Do policemen do their job? I'd discovered that Mike and some of his furtive friends who often went to Fulham, patronised the same programme boy. Did the same, last week, and also bought one from another seller. Saw differences – can't say I've puzzled it out, but there they were. So I dropped my programme in the hope that Hawk-Eye the detective would spot it and wonder what I was up to. Well done, Hawk-Eye! Cipher of some kind, is it?"

"Just pirating," said Roger.

"Oh. Small change." Jeremiah lit a third cigarette. "Anything else I can do for you?"

"Yes," said Roger. "You can tell me whether you know any of these people."

He took several photographs from his desk and pushed them in front of Jeremiah. Among the pictures was one of Maidment and one of Tommy Clayton. Jeremiah pushed Clayton's out of alignment, looked thoughtfully at the others, and then fingered Maidment's.

"I think I've seen him around some place," he said. "Might call him to mind, if it will help. The other cove is Clayton, of course, the know-all of the *Echo*. Man always gets under my skin. He's by way of being a Perriman pet, but I suppose you know that."

Roger said: "How is it *you* know?"

"I patronise Perriman's pets, you never know when they'll come in useful."

"Which Perriman is so fond of Clayton?" demanded Roger.

Jeremiah said: "If you don't know, it wouldn't be hard to find out. It's young Ronald. Ronald is Samuel's eldest son, the white-headed boy of the family. Clayton has a buxom sister, not to say luscious. Ronald is fond of Beryl Clayton. Q.E.D."

"That all you know?" asked Roger.

"Everything," Jeremiah affirmed. "Very bright boy, Clayton, with great ambitions. Why not? Mind if I go now? It's half-past five and I've a lot of work."

"I won't keep you much longer," Roger assured him, and surreptitiously pressed a bell-push fastened beneath the edge of his desk. That was the signal which he had arranged with a sergeant – who was with Sybil Lennox in the next room. "I don't want to exaggerate the dangers of the present position, Scott, but I don't think you fully appreciate them. Several murders have been committed; far too much food is stolen. It must be stamped out. A lot of people who may think they're just helping friends or fallen relatives will probably get hurt if they don't tell the truth."

Jeremiah looked solemn.

"Let that be a lesson to me," he said, pushing his chair back. "You'll do, West."

He stood up, and went to the door. He saw the handle turn and drew back.

The door opened and a man said: "Miss Lennox, sir ..."

Anything else he intended to say was lost in a sharp exclamation from Sybil. She appeared half inside and half out of the room, while Jeremiah stared at her, his smile fading, a hard, bleak expression in his eyes. They eyed each other for some seconds; tense, painful seconds; then Jeremiah shot a searing glance at Roger, and stepped forward, making the girl move to one side.

Chapter Twenty-Eight

News From Afar

Sybil came slowly into the room, without looking back at Jeremiah. She was pale and her hands were trembling. She walked as if she were in pain, and sat down in the chair which Jeremiah had vacated without being invited. Then she looked at Roger with her eyes rounded and showing traces of the shock of that encounter.

"You hate that man, don't you?" demanded Roger.

"I don't—like him."

"You hate him, and you must have reason to hate, and you're frightened of him," said Roger. "Is he one of the men who've forced you to work for them? Are you scared of naming him because of what he might do to you?"

She moistened her lips.

"No—no, I just don't like him. Don't trust him."

"Did his brother work with him?"

"I—I don't know," she said. "It's no use asking me anything about him; I don't *know* more than I've told you."

"All right, Miss Lennox. Have you read through the typewritten copy of the statement you made last night?"

"Yes, and I've signed it."

"You've remembered nothing more?"

"No, nothing. There—isn't any more." She leaned forward now. Her eyes were really lovely, he could well understand how men could fall for her. Was she far more cunning than she appeared – and as Jeremiah seemed to think? "Mr West, I—I would tell you more if I could, I know it's no use holding anything back now, but – everything I know is in that statement."

"Very well," said Roger.

She didn't get up.

Roger said: "Mr Lessing travelled with you?"

"Yes, with—with two policemen." She shivered. "I don't want to go back to Brighton, and I don't want to go to Mrs Clarke. I'm—still so afraid."

"You needn't be," Roger said more gently. "We'll look after you now."

"You didn't before," she reminded him. *"Can't* you keep me here? Safe? *They* can't get at me here; it's the only place where I can rest now."

Of course he could charge her.

It need only be a nominal charge; she could be remanded next day in custody – no magistrate would refuse a remand. And she would be quite safe; she was probably right about the danger, although he had tried to convince himself that 'they' would no longer be interested in her, because they knew that she could no longer be frightened into keeping silent. But he would prefer her to be at large, although closely watched – so that if there were another attack her assailants could be caught.

A telephone bell rang.

He was glad to look away from her as he lifted the receiver.

"West speaking."

"Come along and see me, will you?" asked Chatworth, and his voice was so gruff that Roger felt sure he had more news.

"May I be a few minutes, sir?" asked Roger. "I've someone with me, who—"

"Be as quick as you can," said Chatworth.

The girl had not once looked away from him while he had been talking to Chatworth. He now knew what action to take, the moment of weakness had gone.

"Miss Lennox," he said, "you will have full police protection. I advise you to return to your usual boarding-house in Chelsea. In any case, wherever you go, a police escort will follow you. Now I've urgent business to attend to."

He stood up in a gesture of dismissal.

The girl looked at him with silent reproach, and then turned and limped away.

Mark was waiting for her downstairs. She told him what had happened, and he showed no surprise. Two police-sergeants followed them from Scotland Yard, and one came forward when Mark beckoned from the wheel of his car.

"We're going to my flat," Mark said. "Tell Mr West when you can. And see that it's watched, please."

"Will Miss Lennox be staying there?"

"Yes," said Mark emphatically.

Chatworth was sombre. The *Echo* had brought strong criticism from the Home Office, and they were after someone's scalp. "Have you made any progress, Roger?"

"Not much, it won't surprise me if we get another crop of robberies soon," said Roger. "I've asked the Brighton police to raid Perriman's big wholesale branch there. The report should come through at any time."

"What about other branches?" Chatworth demanded.

"I can't see much point in picking 'em out with a pin," said Roger.

"Had any news about the Perriman Rolls-Royce?"

Roger had to grin.

"There are seven in the family, sir! I've accounted for six, and I'm waiting for a report on Emanuel's, which I'm told is never taken out at night. Meanwhile I'm going to tackle the other football clubs. If the organisation is as big as we fear, hundreds – even thousands – of small operators are in it. They're probably working in cells – one at Fulham, others all over the place. Although there's overall control and direction, each cell will work independently. Probably the one at Fulham has no idea there are others – at the Arsenal and White Hart Lane, for instance. If the show is coming to a head, very soon general orders will be sent out – and that will be on a Saturday. If we could make a simultaneous swoop on them all—"

"Very effective," said Chatworth dryly. "But you're jumping a bit, Roger."

"They must have a means of communicating with their men," said Roger. "I can't think of a better one than the programmes."

"All right, have a shot at it." Chatworth rubbed his chin. "How will you start?"

"I'll get the Fulham people to make inquiries through the London clubs, and visit one or two of the big provincial clubs myself," said Roger.

The Fulham club agreed at once to help.

Roger visited Aston Villa, Newcastle, and Blackpool on a whirlwind tour, and had two long talks by telephone with the manager of Glasgow Rangers.

Most of the clubs were having 'pirate programme' trouble. None of them took it seriously. Such outbreaks came from time to time, and usually faded out because the supporters wouldn't patronise the sellers. In them all were various misprints.

Each had been printed on the same machine, Roger thought, but to satisfy himself, he consulted the master-printer of HM Stationery Office.

"Yes, Inspector," he agreed, "they've been printed on the same machine – a monotype set. You can see from that slightly broken 'e,' the broken tail of the 'g.' But don't be misled by the broken typeface, that's been run off on a new machine."

"How new?" Roger demanded sharply.

"We installed one eighteen months ago," said the master-printer, "we brought it over from America. I doubt if a dozen have been imported since the war, but that's new typeface."

"You're sure that only a few machines have been imported?"

"Quite sure. You're going to the Board of Trade, I suppose, to find out who else has one of them?"

"I am," said Roger firmly.

HM Stationery Office printing works had four of the twelve which had been imported.

Three large printing works had one each. Tucktos had three.

The other two had been installed at the Midlands plant of the Crown Printing & Manufacturing Company – Randall's firm!

Peel, as an inspector of the Board of Trade, was as satisfactory as he had been as a porter at Perriman's Woodhall factory. With him, when he visited the Crown works, was the master-printer, and in a café a mile away on the Solihull Road sat Roger West.

Jim Wilson of Crown showed them round the big machine-room. His gingery hair glistened, his eyes sparkled, he looked to Peel an athletic and nice young man – as he had done to Roger.

He was enthusiastic, as became a man who had only recently become a director. The Crown works had done a wonderful job recently; they had expanded considerably, bought up several smaller firms, and they were by way of competing with the octopus concerns like Tucktos.

He spoke quietly, but managed to make his voice sound above the din of the machines. There were dozens of these, some huge ones and some smaller and, at the far end, the two new monotype machines. They were the latest, from the States – a wonderful job.

Two men sat at the keyboards, typing rapidly.

The master-printer hummed and hawed, said how wonderful it was, could he see some specimens of the typeface? Oh, of course, said Wilson, and sent a boy for some specimens. Wilson took these and began to enthuse.

Peel watched the master-printer.

After a brief inspection, the man nodded meaningly.

Roger saw Peel's car draw up outside the café, and, weary of waiting, hurried out, to the astonishment of a waitress to whom he hadn't yet given an order. One look at Peel told him the result, and, the master-printer said, this could be proved up to the hilt: the programmes had been set on that monotype and printed off on the same machine.

That day, Friday, Roger and Peel returned to the Yard just after half-past five and Roger went straight to the Assistant Commissioner's office.

"This will shake you, sir," said Roger with deep satisfaction. "We've traced the machine, we know who printed and distributed the programmes. I haven't made any arrests yet, I'd rather wait until tomorrow when we've cleared up the gangs at the football grounds, but—"

"Why should this shake me?" asked Chatworth mildly.

Roger laughed.

"The one place we should have looked and didn't, sir – Randall's company. The man concerned is Wilson, one of the directors. He was Randall's friend, or was supposed to be – the man from whom Randall had a letter on the day of his death. Remember?"

Chatworth just stared.

"I've checked very closely," said Roger. "Wilson's very keen on his work and used to be a working printer – as apart from an executive. He spends two or three evenings a week working late on special orders, and a van collects the stuff every Thursday night. It's rumoured that it's private Government work, very hush-hush. No one thinks anything much about it. The night-watchman always see the van off the premises, and I've had a long talk with him. There's been a change of driver lately – and he identified Mike Scott as the driver until a fortnight ago."

"Well, well!" murmured Chatworth.

"Wilson and Scott always left together – the night-watchman understood that the driver gave Wilson a lift home," said Roger. "The van is put in a lock-up garage and the parcels posted from Birmingham Central Post Office early next morning. They're sent all over the country. I've a list of most of the districts, and the country is pretty widely covered – every town where there are 'pirate' programmes gets a parcel. It looked foolproof – it was until we got on to the printers."

"Yes, I suppose so," said Chatworth, "but don't go too fast. Perhaps we've got Wilson but he isn't in this alone."

"Wilson's a football fan," said Roger, rubbing his hands. "Peel got him talking. Spent his boyhood in Fulham, he says, and comes up to every Fulham home match. He'll be at the Cottage tomorrow."

"Or won't he be scared off now?" asked Chatworth.

"Because he knows we're on to the Fulham programmes?" asked Roger. "I don't think so, he'll come to see that everything's all right, I fancy. Remember his London associate can damn him, and he's killed whenever he's in danger. He'll meet his partner tomorrow or I've missed my guess."

"I hope you're right," said Chatworth fervently. "What else? Any idea who his accomplice is?"

"Once we go back to the day of Randall's death," said Roger, "we come to the fact that he got a Perriman order, to Jeremiah Scott's astonishment. Perriman's are involved – someone at Perriman's, anyhow. The director whom Randall saw that day was Samuel Perriman. I should say that Randall tumbled to what was happening, or else knew and wanted an extra cut. He was given the order to placate him, and then bumped off. A talk with Samuel is indicated, but not until after the match. I've an idea that I could get you a centre-stand ticket for the match, sir. Care to come?"

The next morning, James Wilson left his factory a little after nine-thirty, and drove to London. His progress was reported, every two or three miles, by police patrol cars, and one was never far behind him. In London, a police-car – without any tell-tale sign up – followed his gleaming Alvis through the West End and the City, until it stopped near Perriman's Head Office. Wilson did not go into the building, however, but to a popular café nearby, where he was shortly joined by a small, dapper man. It was a quarter-past twelve; they ordered lunch.

A plain-clothes detective sat at the next table, but could not overhear all the conversation although he heard snatches of it, and one sentence impressed itself deeply on his mind.

It was Wilson who uttered it: *"After next week, they won't know whether they're coming or going. This week's show was child's play!"*

This, and other snatches of conversation, were duly reported to Roger at Craven Cottage. He arrived there just after one-thirty, when there were only a few hundred people in the ground.

It soon began to fill up.

Chapter Twenty-Nine

Last Kick-Off

At all the League grounds the crowds thronged to see the last kick-off of the season. There appeared to be no more police than usual, because most were in plain clothes. Several were standing near the turnstiles – not far, in each case, from a seller of 'pirate' programmes.

Inside each ground, there was a peculiar situation near the turnstiles.

There was one programme seller unknown to Fulham officials – the 'pirate.' Every man who bought a programme from the 'pirate' and then paid his money and was clicked through was touched on the shoulder and taken to a large tent which had been erected nearby. Most of them were too astonished to protest. A few tried to get away, but couldn't go back through the turnstile and found every other exit blocked. Only one or two slipped through the police cordon. There were many innocent fans, but no protest availed them. As the time for the kick-off arrived, plain vans drew up, ready to take the men off for interrogation. The guilty would be held, the innocent released with a spate of apologies.

The 'pirate' programme seller stood in a different position near the wharf. He was a little, middle-aged man with a hang-dog look, and was obviously nervous.

In the stand Roger and Chatworth were sitting together. Samuel and Emanuel Perriman were in their usual places. Jeremiah Scott had been quick to see Roger and grin. Peel and other Yard men were near the exit from this block; in the third row, Jim Wilson sat smiling, and next to him was Akerman – the Perriman buyer.

"Everyone here?" demanded Chatworth.

"Yes," said Roger, who could see everyone in whom he was interested. "I wonder if it *is* Akerman of Perriman's we want."

"Looks like it," said Chatworth.

"I'm rather sold on Samuel," said Roger. "I—"

His words were drowned in a roar which greeted the West Bromwich team as the players ran on to the field. Another roar greeted Fulham.

Then suddenly a man appeared at the top of the steps – a little furtive man; the programme seller. Roger stiffened and nudged Chatworth. The programme seller sidled past Peel, who was on duty there, and touched Wilson on the shoulder. Wilson glared at him and waved him away, but the man bent forward and whispered urgently – doubtless telling him what he knew of the detentions.

On the field, the two captains were shaking hands, the referee had a coin poised on his thumb-nail.

The Fulham captain won and indicated the direction he would choose, bringing another roar from the crowd.

Wilson and Akerman jumped up.

Peel and two uniformed constables blocked the exit.

Wilson, who had seen the police, suddenly moved forward, pushing aside two people on the seats in front of him, climbing over the shoulders of the spectators in the next seats in front again, A man protested, but Wilson ignored him and was near the first row. Akerman tried to follow, but Peel grabbed his arm. Now people were standing up in protest. The programme seller ducked and tried to get to the exit, but a policeman held him.

Wilson reached the first row of seats, immediately behind the standing enclosure – no one in front of him had yet seen anything of the disturbance. Roger was already hurrying down the gangway. Wilson sprang down into the enclosure, pushed his way to the railings which guarded the playing pitch, and vaulted over them.

The teams were lined up for the kick-off, the referee had the whistle to his lips.

Roger crashed through the people in the enclosure and cleared the railings. Wilson looked round, saw him, and then rushed straight on to the pitch. The whistle blew, the ball was swung out to the wing. A roar of protest boomed out as people saw Wilson, then Roger, invade the pitch. Two or three uniformed policemen followed, looking ungainly. The ball passed Wilson and came straight at Roger.

He kicked it out of his path and sent it ballooning up into the air, bringing an ironic cheer. The referee blew his whistle shrilly, but Wilson went straight across the pitch, with Roger only a few yards behind him.

Wilson snatched something out of his pocket and turned round. Roger saw a yellow flash and then heard the report. It silenced the crowd.

The bullet missed Roger. Several of the players who had started after Wilson backed away when they saw the gun. Policemen near the touchlines were closing in, but there was a wide gap – a gap through which Wilson hoped to pass. If he once got into the crowd on the main terrace, he might get away.

He fired again.

Roger felt a sharp pain in his right arm, but it didn't slow him down.

Wilson was only a few yards from the touchline now, with a dozen police some distance away. Then a slim, dark-haired figure in white moved forward swiftly, went down in a flying tackle and caught Wilson's ankles. Wilson turned the gun on him and fired. The report was loud – and followed by a mighty roar of anger. But Wilson went over, the gun slid from his grip, and Roger pounced.

Wilson butted at him with his head, catching him on the jaw. Roger struck him beneath the chin and then saw policemen looming above him and heard a man say: "Okay, sir."

Roger looked round anxiously at the Fulham player, who was on his feet and smiling broadly. The crowd's roar of relief was like thunder, and it followed Roger, Wilson, and the police as they turned to recross the field.

Chatworth, Roger, and Peel were with Wilson, Akerman, and the programme seller in the boardroom of the Cottage. The crowd was roaring outside, rattles were going and bells were ringing.

Peel sat at a table, with a notebook open.

Wilson, his hair ruffled and his chin bruised, stood by the window with an ugly scowl on his face. The contents of his pockets were on the table in neat array, and the gun, with a label already attached, lay with them. So far he had refused to make a statement. The programme seller had made a halting confession mingled with details; he had no idea Wilson had a gun, he wouldn't have worked for a killer; he was a pal of Maidment; the original programme seller had been his son. He knew his son was dead; thought it was an accident, he didn't believe he had been murdered.

But it was obvious that he did, and equally obvious that he did not know a great deal.

He had attended every home match, watched his son, and been told by Maidment to warn Wilson and Akerman if the police were ever interested in the programmes. He'd seen one man who had run from the police that afternoon, realised what was afoot, and carried out his instructions. He had a pass to the stands, which had been supplied by Maidment.

Now Roger, whose wound was only a graze, turned to Wilson.

"You know the game's up," he said. "We've arrested every one of your men on the ground, and on all the other grounds. We know you send orders through programmes, that you were planning a bigger raid next week – and it won't come off. You were caught red-handed in attempted murder, and the only way you might help yourself is to make a full confession."

Wilson's bloodshot eyes looked wild.

"If you've got to have it the hard way, I'll work on you later," said Roger. He turned to Akerman. "Well? You ready to talk?"

Akerman licked his lips.

"If you—" began Wilson.

"Queen's Evidence might help you," Roger said.

Wilson turned away contemptuously; Akerman began to talk in slow, hesitating sentences; Peel's pencil moved rapidly over the pages in his notebook.

Neither Clayton nor Jeremiah Scott were involved, and Perriman's had been unaware of what Akerman had been doing.

Akerman had worked with Wilson almost from the beginning. Their motive was simply profit. Up and down the country wholesale and big retail shops were stocked with stolen foods. Other huge stocks were ready for unloading.

The programme code had been Wilson's idea. Each member of the gang who went to Fulham games had a key-list of shops, factories, and warehouses which were to be robbed, and the misspellings and misprints in the League Tables told the men – each of whom had a number – which places to raid and where to take the stolen goods. The League I Table named the victims, League II the places to which the stolen goods were to be taken. Akerman, chief buyer for the Perriman branches and who knew many of the managers, had gradually compiled a list of the managers who would help in distribution and store 'hot' goods.

The method was simple in outline, complicated in operation – but each man who bought a programme and had the key to the code knew exactly what he was to do. His money for his previous job was folded in the programme. Only those who gave a code word received a money programme, of course. His responsibility ended when his job was done. Very few men knew who else worked with the organisation – the cell system had been brought to perfection.

Sybil Lennox's part the police already knew.

Mike Scott had been fairly prominent in the organisation, and knew that Akerman was involved. He had arranged to get the drawings of places to be raided from Sybil, had blackmailed her into continuing with the work when she knew the truth about it. Little Relf had also known – and it was Wilson who, in touch with all developments by telephone, had arranged for Kirby and Relf to be killed. Wilson had actually been near Wignall's garage on the night of the raid there, and had sent the two masqueraders on to the roof to finish off Relf. The smaller fry were mostly habitual criminals.

Maidment had been so closely followed by Clayton that Clayton had been kidnapped. Maidment had weakened, been killed, and his body had been burnt at the dump by the second Relf, who was now under arrest. They kept Clayton for questioning.

Peel had been attacked because Relf was scared of being suspected of the murder.

The investigation had started, so far as the police were concerned, with a simple mistake.

When Randall had called on Samuel Perriman, the director had sent for the specimen file. Earlier that day, Akerman had been looking through the copy for a programme from Fulham, to be sent to Wilson for printing. He'd been interrupted and slipped the draft programme inside the file. That had been put away, and he couldn't remember where he had put the draft. Afterwards, the copy – typewritten – had been included with the specifications which Randall had taken away with him. He had carried it about in the brief-case. There was, in addition to the 'copy,' a note from Akerman to Wilson. Had Randall read this, he would have known something of the organisation, and could have betrayed everything to the police.

Akerman had remembered where he'd put it and telephoned Wilson, who had ordered Randall's death, which Kirby had carried out. Randall had been followed most of the afternoon, but there'd been no chance to snatch the brief-case. Wilson was afraid that he'd read the letter and programme, hence the murder.

Once police inquiries about Randall's murder started, Wilson had tried to implicate Sybil, hoping that the police would believe all had not been well between her and Randall. Finding that the police were not fooled, Wilson had arranged for her to be implicated further, by planting the brief-case and some of the dummy samples in her room. She only knew Mike Scott and some of the lesser men in the organisation; she could do no great damage even if caught.

Mike Scott had been the London chief operative. All the men highly placed in the organisation knew the risk of being caught and were well paid – but Mike gambled and squandered his money and was usually hard up. He always presented himself to Jeremiah as a victim of circumstances; Jeremiah had believed that and had tried to help him. Jeremiah also blamed Sybil, believing that Mike spent much of his money on her; that explained his dislike of the girl.

Sybil had been kidnapped and questioned because Wilson feared she had learned more from Randall, who could have told her by telephone or at dinner; that was why Mike Scott had tried to kill her. Her questioners were already picked up; so was the manager of the Brighton Perriman's.

Akerman had been in the Rolls-Royce, and had arranged to meet the youth who came by cab. Others, lying in wait, had picked up the youth and killed him simply because, like his father, he knew Wilson by name. A police patrol car, not far away, had forced them to abandon the cab.

Within three days of the mass arrests and the great splash made by the Press about the police 'triumph,' all the hoards of stolen food were discovered.

On the fourth evening, when most of the details were cleared up, Roger reached Bell Street a little after seven o'clock. Janet was in the kitchen, taking his supper out of the oven.

"Darling, I've some news for you. Jack Goodwin left hospital today."

"That's wonderful!" Roger exclaimed, and meant it.

They went into the dining-room, where Janet ate a salad and Roger his share of the midday lunch, warmed up.

"Oh yes," said Janet, "and Mark's coming round tonight. He wondered if you'd mind if he brought Sybil. I said of course you wouldn't, and I want to see what she's like, anyhow. *Is* she good enough for him, darling?"

"Erring child and all that kind of thing, but I don't think Mark will make a mistake."

The front-door bell rang.

"There they are!" exclaimed Janet. "They're nearly an hour early. Darling, finish that quickly, I'll keep them in the sitting-room."

She hurried out, leaving Roger smiling with the knife and fork in his hand. He heard the front door open, and a man's voice – not Mark's. He put down his knife and fork, as Jeremiah Scott said: "He'll spare me a minute, Mrs West, and I don't mind waiting."

Roger went on with his supper.

He kept Jeremiah twelve and a half minutes, and when he went into the sitting-room, found the Tucktos man sitting back in an easy chair, smoking, and holding his cigarette-case between his long fingers. He gave his sardonic grin as Roger entered and sat up. He opened the case.

"Not smoking too much now, are you?"

"No," said Roger. "Thanks. And to what, as they say, do we owe this honour?"

"I've always wanted to see a policeman in his moment of triumph," said Jeremiah. "Congratulations."

"Thanks. But what do you really want?"

"You never were easily satisfied," said Jeremiah. He was suddenly grave; he didn't find this easy. "As a matter of fact, West, I've just seen my brother. He's told me the whole truth – in front of a police witness, so I'm doing no harm. Sybil Lennox wasn't his downfall. Instead, he was nearly hers. I've been hard on the girl. Wanted to make it clear that it was a case of misunderstanding. I've nothing personally against her. Nice creature, in the right hands, I fancy. Might tell her that I said so."

Roger said: "Yes, I will, gladly."

"Thanks. On the whole, a very nice job for you," said Scott. "Seen Clayton lately, by the way?"

"No."

"He's feeling a bit under the weather. He and I were in cahoots at one time, trying to discover what really went on. I knew there was some funny business; wanted to help Mike, and thought that Sybil was indirectly responsible for Randall's death. So Tommy and I teamed up. I knew he thought Perriman's dock-side warehouse was being used, that's why I was there that night."

"The truth will out," said Roger dryly.

"Matter of timing," said Jeremiah.

"It nearly got time for you," retorted Roger, and Jeremiah laughed as he stood up. But the laughter rang hollow and it was a dejected man who left the house.

John Creasey

Gideon's Day

Gideon's day is a busy one. He balances family commitments with solving a series of seemingly unrelated crimes from which a plot nonetheless evolves and a mystery is solved.

One of the most senior officers within Scotland Yard, George Gideon's crime solving abilities are in the finest traditions of London's world famous police headquarters. His analytical brain and sense of fairness is respected by colleagues and villains alike.

> 'The finest of all Scotland Yard series' – New York Times.

Gideon's Fire

Commander George Gideon of Scotland Yard has to deal successively with news of a mass murderer, a depraved maniac, and the deaths of a family in an arson attack on an old building south of the river. This leaves little time for the crisis developing at home ....

> 'Gideon of Scotland Yard emerges as one of the most real working detectives in modern fiction.... A sympathetic and believable professional policeman.' - New York Times

JOHN CREASEY

THE CREEPERS

"The prisoner's hand was thin and bony ... And in the centre of the palm was a pinkish mark. It was the shape of a wolf's head, mouth open, fangs showing. Although it was what he had expected to see, Inspector West felt a twinge of repugnance a stab not unrelated to fear. It was the fifth time he had seen the mark of the wolf – the mark of Lobo."

A gang of cat burglars led by Lobo cause mayhem as they terrorize the city. They must be stopped, but with little in the way of evidence the police are baffled. Just how can Inspector West manage to do this in what is a race against time before more victims succumb?

"Here is an excellent novel of law enforcement officers, harried, discouraged and desperately fatigued, moving inexorably ahead under the pressure of knowledge that they must succeed to save human lives." - Cleveland Plain-Dealer

"Furiously exciting" - Chicago Tribune

"The action is fast, continuous and exciting" - San Francisco News

JOHN CREASEY

THE HOUSE OF THE BEARS

Standing alone in the bleak Yorkshire Moors is Sir Rufus Marne's 'House of the Bears'. Dr. Palfrey is asked to journey there to examine an invalid - who has now disappeared. Moreover, Marne's daughter lies terribly injured after a fall from the minstrel's gallery which Dr. Palfrey discovers was no accident. He sets out to investigate and the results surprise even him . . . .

> *"'Palfrey' and his boys deserve to take their places among the immortals." - Western Mail*

INTRODUCING THE TOFF

Whilst returning home from a cricket match at his father's country home, the Honourable Richard Rollison - alias The Toff - comes across an accident which proves to be a mystery. As he delves deeper into the matter with his usual perseverance and thoroughness , murder and suspense form the backdrop to a fast moving and exciting adventure.

'The Toff has been promoted to a place of honour among amateur detectives.' – The Times Literary Supplement

Printed in Great Britain
by Amazon